Jill Ann

This is my account of my adventures in Hefnerland. I have, however, changed the names of many of the participants out of respect for their feelings.

This book is neither endorsed, nor sponsored by, nor affiliated with Playboy Enterprises Inc. or Hugh M. Hefner. Playboy®, Playmate of the year® and Playmate of the month® Hugh M. Hefner, HMH, Miss January, Miss February, Miss March, Miss April, Miss May, Miss June, Miss July, Miss August, Miss September, Miss October, Miss November, Miss December, Playmate, PMOY, Centerfold, are registered trademarks of Playboy Enterprises International, Inc., all pending or registered in U.S. Patent and Trademark Office.

ISBN 1-58961-171-3

Jill Ann

Upstairs

One Playboy Bunny's Intimate,
Step-by-Step Discovery of the
Playboy Mansion and
What Hef's Really Got Going on Upstairs

by

JILL ANN SPAULDING

It's sad when you think of her wasted life,
For Youth cannot mate with Age.
And her beauty was sold
For an old man's gold.
She's a bird in a gilded cage.

By Virginia

It's like a pinup girl version of Survivor.

Bruce (friend)

Well...I read your book — cover to cover. Wow...I had no idea!! I couldn't put the book down.

Kimmie (girlfriend) California

I read your book - wow!! I couldn't put it down. I'm sending it to my niece. I believe it will be an eye opener for her. As it was for me. You are truly my idol! Congratulations on the book and thank you from not just women but everyone all over. You are proof that "Real" people can live in this world and not compromise their morals. Thanks again!

Katrina, Security Las Vegas

It was impossible to put down. I was impressed by you and your ultimate message. I really think you have something very special here, not simply in the enlightening character of your book and its message, but in the strength of character you exhibit throughout.

To me, yours is a very serious book with an important story to tell to all women about character, image, self-respect and the egotistical exploitation of the false over the true.

Jill Ann, I loved your book for a variety of reasons, but primarily because it is a story about 'True' character overcoming and emerging victorious over 'False' character. In that sense, your focus should remain upon the dynamics between you and Hefner. You, and what you represent are the most important part of this message. Your True character is the heroine of this story.

Tom Wilson of the legendary cartoon character Ziggy
Character Matters
President

*Jill Ann Spaulding's book "**Jill Ann: Upstairs**" is a much deeper and more personal account of her life than the book cover photos might indicate. Once you get past some of the shocking revelations of life at the Playboy Mansion - you will find a tale of a young woman caught up in chasing her own dreams and finding it wasn't entirely what she had bargained for. Her story takes us on her search for meaning and understanding in world that few know anything about. The choices she makes and the people she meets along the way make this more than just a sexual tale of misdeeds and exploitations—this book is truly a personal journey of inner discovery. Her experiences become an epiphany which causes her to reflect on the true destination of her life path. Her warnings at the end of the book are sober reminders of the dangers and the seriousness of what she saw.*

W.H. McDonald Jr.
President of the American Authors' Association
Award winning poet and author

Not a single dull page. Nicely done;-)

Alex Mandossian
www.askmylist.com California

I found your story fascinating. Getting out from under Hef's domination was a good thing for you. You saved your pride, your integrity, and you learned you can survive and flourish by being free, rather than living in thrall to a man whose apparent sole interest in life is in possessing people as though they were play things.

Lou Krieger
Author of Seven great poker books
www.loukriger.com

Dedication

This book is dedicated to Bruce Gifford, my best friend, and companion who stood by me through it all.

"All Profits from the purchase of this book will be donated to Prehab. Org."

WWW.PREHAB.ORG - PREHAB of Arizona's mission is Helping Families...Changing lives.

PREHAB provides both PREvention and reHABilitation services with our Domestic Violence, Homeless and Youth programs. Each night we are licensed for up to 300 people to sleep in one of our homes or shelters.- Our 17 different programs in the Phoenix Area help thousands of individuals each year facing behavioral, social and economic challenges.-- We are a catalyst for people to change.

Two goals for our clients are:
*- - to feel hopeful and develop a sense of their own value and strength
*- - to strengthen the skills necessary to create, communicate and carry out decisions to meet life goals.

Prologue

Kelly whispered to me, "Hef would like you to come upstairs with him and his girlfriends when we get back to the mansion."

"He said that to me when we were dancing, but I didn't know what would happen for sure."

"He really likes you. You're so beautiful and nice. I wish you were one of them."

"Well, if I become an official girlfriend I'll ask them to invite you every time we go out."

She was incredulous. "Really?"

"Yes. You're so nice and fun. You're terrific." Kelly was so enthused she was smiling from ear to ear.

She said, "When you get back to the mansion you won't have to do anything. You can just watch. You don't have to participate. I'll guide you through the entire time, and I'll be with you all the way. Hef told me personally to take care of you."

I was unbelievably excited to find out what happened "upstairs"—this mythical place of legend. I had no idea what to expect.

I was excited and very curious. We all left the club and I was ushered into Hef's luxurious limousine—designed to get us noticed. I noticed Hef passing out a pill of some kind to his girlfriends in the limo. In a whisper, I asked Kelly what he was giving them, and she said I had to be an official girlfriend before I would get one. The limo headed back to the mansion. Expensive champagne flowed, and girls, one dressed sexier than the next and all voluptuous, were hanging all over Hef. The music was so intense that I could feel the base shaking my whole body. The flashing lights inside the limo made me feel like I was on a disco floor. We pulled up to the outside gates of the back of mansion, got out, and proceeded to walk up the long mansion drive in the dark, and headed in through the mansion's front door and all walked up the stairs.

The girls went in different directions—not straight into Hef's bedroom. Kelly took me quickly through a very large walk-in closet filled with Hef's pajamas, memorabilia, pictures and tons of clothing. We walked through quickly, but I tried to look around. The whole mansion was like no place I had ever been before, and I was awed by all of the items in the closet. Kelly went to a section in the closet where many nicely cleaned pink pajamas hung as she handed me a set on a hanger.

Then she led me to a gigantic marble bathtub.

"First, you have to take a bath."

I felt scared. Kelly saw it in my eyes.

"Don't worry," she said. "You only have to participate if you want to. It's hilarious and you won't ever forget it. When you're older you can write a book!"

She took off her clothes and started to run the water in the tub. I slowly removed my jewelry and shoes.

While the warm water ran, she started to whisper quietly to me as she helped me undo my dress.

"We're going to go in and sit on the bed. If you don't want to participate just keep your bottoms on. Otherwise, take them off. I'll be with you the entire time, and we'll stay together. I'm going to pretend to give you oral sex and you can touch me, or kiss me or whatever you're comfortable doing. All the girls will be around us doing the same thing. They're all faking it. No one is bisexual so don't touch another girl unless she touches you. If you watch you'll be able to tell that they're totally acting—nothing is really going on. Just follow my lead and you'll be fine."

I started to relax. In my mind, I talked to myself. I knew it. *I knew it. I can do this. I can pretend to kiss another girl. No problem. I can handle this. He probably just sits there and watches all of us,* I thought to myself. I assumed it was all for show, like a put-on private striptease. On some level, I naively thought it was about showing off our bodies, but not actually *doing* anything sexual.

A girl named Amber came into the bathroom and asked us what we wanted to drink. I ordered a Diet Coke® and Malibu. Kelly had the same. Kelly was now in the bathtub, washing herself with sexy-smelling soap. She got out of the tub, and a girl named Britney got in. This was a cleansing ritual done by every girl invited upstairs. All the official girlfriends were supposed to be doing the same thing in their own personal bathrooms.

Deborah came into the bathroom and did not look thrilled to see me. I didn't want to get my hair wet and Kelly diffused the situation by asking if

Deborah had a hair clip. Deborah gave me one, and I thanked her over and over again. Deborah was near the sink with a stack of thick fluffy hand towels, and she was soaking them in water and ringing them out before placing them in a bowl.

"What am I supposed to do?" I asked as I got into the tub.

"Wash under your arms, privates, and elsewhere, just like a regular bath."

"This isn't regular for me."

Suddenly Hef came into the bathroom with a camera. I felt a little shocked, and Kelly asked if it was okay if he took a picture. I said, "Sure." He took a picture of Britney and me naked in the tub.

All of the girls seemed to have vanished, and it was just Kelly and me in the bathroom together. I went to the restroom and took my time. I was very nervous. Amber came rushing in and told us to hurry up; everyone was waiting for us. Kelly grabbed my hand and led me into the main bedroom of Hugh Hefner. It was very dark. The only light came from two gigantic big screen TVs. Extremely loud techno music was playing.

I had made it. This was The Mansion. This was Hugh Hefner. This was my dream. This was Upstairs.

Introduction

I've always been an open-minded individual. I guess it's because I was raised by liberal parents from the 1970s, I was privy to the magazines my grandparents and my boyfriend subscribed to—*Playboy*—and the *Playboy* channel on television. Why would a girl like me buy *Playboy* and let my boyfriend read it? And why would I let him watch the channel?

"Tell them they can't have it, and they'll want it all the more," my mother always said.

I'm sure she was not talking about this subject, but I used this advice in my everyday life. On some level, I guess I thought that men with girlfriends and wives who forbid them from looking at *Playboy* would then sneak around to look at it—or worse . . . they'd cheat. I intended my relationships to be based on trust. Of course, like many people, I thought *Playboy* was classy, upscale, and acceptable. Anything else was porn. *Playboy* featured the women like gorgeous art, airbrushed to perfection, with taste and style. The lighting was always sexy, not harsh. They were like paintings brought to life.

In the 1960s when women were more voluptuous and zaftig, they reminded me of Renaissance oil paintings. I had always dreamed of being a *Playboy* centerfold, and if it was good enough for me to have been willing to do it, then the magazine was okay for my boyfriend to read. Besides, my grandpa was a *Playboy* collector and proud of it. He had read *Playboy* as far back as I could remember. I think that was one of the biggest reasons I wanted to be a Playmate. Of course, my grandpa made it very plain he did not want to see his sweet granddaughter nude. However, he thought the magazine was great, and my grandma always said Hugh Hefner's publication had the most beautiful girls in the world. They allowed me to look at the magazines as far back as I can remember, and to be honest, they *were* the most beautiful girls in the world, as far as I could see.

I started collecting autographed *Playboy* covers. My first signed *Play-*

boy was bought at a memorabilia store in Harrah's Casino. Drew Barrymore was the featured star. The very next day, my boyfriend and I purchased a gigantic framed collection of four different covers of Jenny McCarthy, that sexy and outrageous blonde, all autographed and another of her signing a Playboy book. The collection grew to be huge with seventy-six, very well-known autographed covers from Madonna, Vanna White, and all ten of Pamela Anderson's appearances in the pages, as well as Anna Nicole Smith, Bo Derek, Caprice, Claudia Schiffer, Sharon Stone, and many others. I became obsessed with the collection. I had an eight-foot by eight-foot, air-brushed *Playboy* bunny mounted in my pool/bar room. I had pool sticks with *Playboy* bunnies and playmates on the handles, a cue ball with the bunny; the entire room was filled with bunny glasses, napkins, and a large street sign that read "Honorary Hugh Hefner Way." Everything was *Playboy*, and I loved it. It was a great hobby. I would surf Ebay for hours and bid for celebrity signed covers and *Playboy* memorabilia.

My boyfriend was the hero in all this collecting. Anyone who came into our house would tell him "*You're the Man!*" Not only for having a girlfriend who liked *Playboy* but who allowed him to have a subscription and the *Playboy* channel. During every party, Bruce would turn on the television to show all of the guys and women how lucky he was. Every woman wanted to know which cover I was on, what month I appeared, etc. I felt so beautiful and loved all the attention, even though I had never appeared and had never posed nude. Everyone assumed I had been in it because I had that classic *Playboy* bunny "look."

So how did this wonderful collection of mine that I worked so hard to get, so hard to have—each and every cover custom framed and mounted—turn sour? How did it happen that when I put my house up for sale, I put it up as completely furnished leaving the new owner with the entire seventy-six-picture collection? All the *Playboy* memorabilia, including my first personal letter from Hef, autographed with pictures and framed, were eventually auctioned off, placed on Ebay® and for little to no money without a care.

Hugh Hefner arriving with his blondes in tow at Glamourcon October 21st, 2000. A media and Paparazzi frenzy.

Blondes arriving with Hugh Hefner and posing for pictures for the Media and Paparazzi.

Hugh Hefner

Chapter One

It all started when I arrived at the ripe age of thirty. A woman's worst nightmare: getting old. One day that look in the mirror will prove the dreaded evidence that all those childhood dreams of being an actress, model, or someone famous could not be realized. I had put all those dreams and fantasies aside when I was twenty-one while I pursued a successful career as an owner of a chain of clothing stores. It was true that I had a beautiful four-thousand square foot house that was completely paid for, great cars, furnishings, financial success, and the admiration of my employees. It wasn't enough. The one dream that stood out the most was being a *Playboy* centerfold.

It wasn't just that I was getting older . . . it was a turning point. I wanted to do something special. Maybe for someone else this moment happens when turning forty. Maybe someone else might want to climb a mountain, enter a marathon, bungee jump or skydive. Fly to Paris. But I had all the material possessions I wanted. I wanted to do something so that when I was *sixty*, I could look back and say, "See what I did!"

I was in the poolroom amongst all my *Playboy* memorabilia when it hit me. I was going to do it. It wasn't too late. I decided I needed a strategy. I was a businesswoman. I could do this. I applied all the common sense and drive that had taken me to where I was to the goal of being a *Playmate*. I realized that at thirty, realistically I had only a very remote chance of being a *Playmate*. I researched about a year of *Playboy* magazines and found that the oldest one was about twenty-six. If I were going to have a chance of achieving my goal, being four years older than the average, I would have to really look terrific. I would have to have an edge, the look, the figure, the personality—everything.

For starters, I would need someone teach me to do my makeup. I never really wore makeup through high school and still didn't, just a little blush and mascara. I was going to need to look the part. A model friend of mine gave me a list of makeup artists, and I called the one she recommended the most. I told the makeup artist that I had just turned thirty and wanted to look younger, sexier—more "*Playboy*-ish."

When she came to our house, my boyfriend Bruce videotaped the makeup session so I could watch it over and over again to learn the techniques. Within a week, I threw out all the old makeup I had and purchased everything new from different stores all over town. It cost hundreds of dollars, but I was thrilled with my new look. I watched the video daily. I was on the way to a new me!

Flipping through a local paper I came across an ad for a personal trainer. To get the look I wanted, dedication was the name of the game. I had already had breast surgery a few years before, and they were perky and beautiful. My teeth were perfect from having braces as a child. I had great legs, outstanding breasts, was thin and a natural blonde. Through the years, many friends had already told me I should send my pictures in to *Playboy*. Many people thought I was a model.

If I was in danger of being automatically dismissed because of my age, I also needed a gimmick. *Playboy* often featured women who were firefighters, police officers, featured on a reality show . . . women who were some sort of celebrity or who had something unusual about themselves or their career. I was none of these—but I had been playing Texas Holdem on nearly a daily basis for over eight years. So I hatched a plan: Get in shape and send in my pictures and tell them that I was a tournament poker player. If they had a rule on age limit for being a *Playmate*, then they could do a poker article on me like they do the firefighters and police gals.

I tried not to get depressed and started reflecting on other people's ages. Thirty was the old twenty, and forty was the old thirty. People were exercising and staying in shape . . . the old definitions of sexy were flying out the window. People over thirty at the time were very popular. Jennifer Lopez, thirty-one; Lucy Liu, thirty-three; Faith Hill, thirty-four; Nicole Kidman, thirty-four; Ashley Judd, thirty-three; Gwyneth Paltrow; twenty-nine; Sarah Jessica Parker, star of the sexiest show on television, thirty-four; Julia Roberts, America's biggest females star, thirty-four; Cameron Diaz, twenty-nine. I took heart that the last playmate was twenty-nine (Tina Marie Jordan). The stars of "Beverly Hills 90210" were also no longer high school kids. Tori Spelling was thirty, Jason Priestley was thirty-three, Jennie Garth was thirty-one, and so on. No, I told myself, I was *not* too old!

The personal trainer came out to the house. I didn't tell him about my plans for *Playboy*. I'm not sure if I told him that I wanted to look like a

Playmate, but I did say I wanted lean muscles, great curves—not bulky. I was feeling good. My trainer had me on a special diet. By the time he was through, I felt I was ready. The only things I didn't like were my thighs. No matter what I tried, they didn't change. Most women, I suppose, have that *one* body part they're displeased with. I knew that, realistically speaking, 99 percent of women would have been thrilled to look like I did, but I wanted nothing but a lean, mean, sexy body, and I continued to complain. The trainer continued to make me do more and more exercises.

Finally, point blank he said, "You're thirty. You're never going to have the body you did at twenty."

I was devastated. I wanted *Playboy* to have no excuse except my age. Because I had already undergone breast surgery a few years before, I guess for me, plastic surgery did not seem like a drastic option. I sincerely believed if there was something you did not like about yourself, and you had the power to change it through modern medicine, you should. I went to a local doctor in Arizona, even though I was 115 pounds and 14 percent body fat. I showed him what I didn't like. I told him flat-out what my plan was. He suggested inner and outer liposuction. I figured that, while I was at it, I would get larger implants. I had to stand out—not freaky—but I had to have an edge over the hundreds of other twenty-four-year-old girls who get implants. I also asked about my lips. The doctor said that he could weave a rope to the upper and lower lips to make them slightly fuller. I added that procedure to the list.

In one day, my thighs were slimmed, both lips were fuller, and my breasts doubled in size. The pain was incredible. My lips were so swollen I looked like a monkey. I could not lie on either side and wore spandex pants for optimum results. I didn't tell anyone in my family that I was having this done and, until this book I have never admitted to the liposuction. After about a month, the doctor determined that an uneven amount had been removed from my legs. He would redo it at no charge. The second surgery was the very worst, and I was in twice the pain. The medical team told me they could give me more pain reliever at the office, or I could make my way home to take my own medication. I decided on the latter, which was a big mistake. I couldn't work out for six months . . . the recovery was much harder than I expected.

The waiting began. My age clock continued ticking away. I maintained my diet and spent time working on and preparing my plan. When the time came for my trainer to return, he couldn't believe what I'd done. He worked with me for two months getting into the shape I wanted for my first photos to be submitted to *Playboy*. As a final touch, I went through the very painful procedure of Botox. (This is to remove all wrinkles from forehead or eye area, or wherever you put the painful injection. It paralyzes this section of your face so that there will be no wrinkles. Many of the movie stars use this to look much younger.)

Before I was completely ready to send pictures to *Playboy*, an event called Glamourcon came up October 21 to 22, 2000. It is a gathering of models—mainly *Playboy* models and Playmates. I decided I would attend. I was very excited to go to Los Angeles. I wanted to check out the competition, of course, but I would also get to meet Hugh Hefner who sometimes makes an appearance the first day of the event. I met many of the current Playmates and some of the older ones. I had a picture taken with Hugh Hefner, and he signed my birthday issue, Playboy April 1970 "To Jill. Love, Hugh Hefner." I was thrilled. I had finally met the most powerful man in the *Playboy* business—the *Playboy* icon himself. He came in with an entourage of blondes, all of whom I assumed were Playmates. The girls had on the shortest shorts; sexy jeans, little tank tops and t-shirts, and they all had their hair and makeup done to perfection.

The media frenzy was unbelievable. Everyone was taking pictures and standing in line for autographs. The thing that impressed me the most was that he took time throughout the room to greet many of the girls from past *Playboy* years, giving them big hugs and thanking them. It seemed like such a family atmosphere. It seemed as if he was paternal almost, caring about each girl in his *Playboy* empire.

I could feel the excitement—the glitz—in the air. I wanted to be part of it. Hef was there only a short time and left with all the blondes in tow. The best thing was almost everyone there thought I was a Playmate just stopping by to visit the others. I was both flattered and motivated. I met a Playmate named Suzi Simpson who asked me what month I was.

"Oh, no . . . I'm just here getting autographs, and I wanted to meet Hugh Hefner."

"You're kidding. You are definitely Playmate material."

I was fishing for information. "You think I should send my pictures to the magazine?"

"Absolutely not! What you want to do is go directly to Santa Monica. They test for Playmates on Thursdays, and you need to call them and make an appointment. Tell them I sent you."

I was breathless. "Thank you so much!" Prior to going to L.A., I didn't know about this test, so this was a big leg up on my list toward my goal. I felt like nothing could stop me now.

*Hugh Hefner signing my
Playboys that I personally
handed him.*

*Hugh Hefner and
Playmate Buffy
Tyler autographing.*

Platinum Blondes

Chapter Two

It took a while to get an appointment in Santa Monica because there were so many people on the list. I had maintained my workouts and diet, and I finally got my opportunity for my first test on December 7, 2000—about two months after my trip to L.A.

Before I arrived, I had the works: manicure, pedicure, hair, facial, bikini wax, and a fresh fake tan for the perfect glow. I arrived dressed in a pink sequined tube top, black cloth pants that hugged my body, sexy black heels, and a white fluffy cropped jacket that had an almost Marilyn Monroe aura about it. I signed in, and they gave me a test application. I provided the following information: Measurements 38-25-35, 118 pounds, 5 feet 7 inches tall, blonde, blue eyes, 30 years of age, no piercings (including ears), no tattoos, and was currently a resale clothing shop owner. I wrote that my hobbies were poker and playing with my beloved poodle. I purposely did not mention too much about the poker because I was trying out for Playmate, and if I didn't make it I would try a different approach.

I was called in for the test shots. I met with one of the official *Playboy* photographers. They walked me past many gigantic pictures of famous *Playboy* covers and Playmates (Pamela Anderson, Jenny McCarthy, and Anna Nicole Smith.) It was like a museum. My heart was pounding—excited and scared. This would be the first time I had ever posed nude, but I felt confident that my hard work and cosmetic surgery would pay off. The photographer led me into a room, told me to put on the silky robe hanging by the door and to come out when I was ready. He led me into a small, dimly lit room for the shoot.

After about eight Polaroid shots in a variety of positions, all designed to imitate the poses you see in *Playboy* all the time—some with that sort of "peek-a-boo" playfulness, I said, "It's so hot today. My makeup is almost gone."

"It's better with less makeup. That way they can see you raw. Don't worry about it. You're perfect—absolutely gorgeous!"

"Oh, you say that to all the girls."

"Really, I don't," he said.

I must have smiled a mile wide. He wanted me to look at the pictures. I didn't want to and just glanced quickly at them.

"We'll be calling you for sure either tomorrow or first thing Monday."

"Really?"

He smiled and nodded.

I changed back into my clothes and headed out to the car where Bruce was waiting. I talked all the way back to the hotel. I was sure that, with the photographer being so confident, I would make it. I was on cloud nine and had no intention of getting off quickly. My cell phone went with me everywhere.

Friday went by. The weekend dragged. Monday I was so nervous I was afraid to answer it if it did ring. By Wednesday the 13th with no call, I called the Santa Monica office. I spoke to Tashanna Williams in Playmate Submissions and told her what the photographer had said.

"Our procedure is to send out a letter," she explained.

"But the photographer seemed very sure that they would call me directly."

"I'm sorry. I don't know what to tell you."

While waiting for the letter I decided to e-mail Suzi Simpson, Miss January 1992, and contacted her via e-mail on December 13, 2000. I brought her up to speed on the week's events and wondered if that had been her experience as well.

On Wednesday the 20th I received a letter: it basically told me that though the photos were good, they only select twelve centerfolds a year—from thousands of girls—and I didn't make it. They reminded me how tough the competition was and signed off pleasantly.

The letter was written the same day I had called her. I didn't understand. The photographer was so positive. What had happened between him and the editors? Was it only his opinion? Naturally, I was already concerned about my age and that was the first thing that came to mind. The photographer did not return my data sheet when I left. Maybe he was sure I was perfect but when the editors noticed I was thirty, they decided to pass. I decided to write Tashanna back.

I received my regret letter on December 19th turning my application down. I was wondering if there was a special edition or lingerie I could do? I had left it blank where the application asked what I was applying for because I was open to anything Playboy would want me for. Can I have those pictures back to forward to a different department or is this decision final for anything with Playboy? I met ...Suzi Simpson, Kimberly Donley and Barbara Moore back in October and they all thought I would be perfect... I know you must have a million people call and write you ... Please fax or mail back a response or advice. You can also reach me on my cell.

She called me back. "The editors said that even for special editions or lingerie they were not interested at this time. I'm sorry."

I was back to square one. But I also know any dream worth having is worth pursuing to the fullest.

Young modeling dreams, striking a pose with my bunny!

Growing up in Granite Falls Washington already with the bunny by my side.

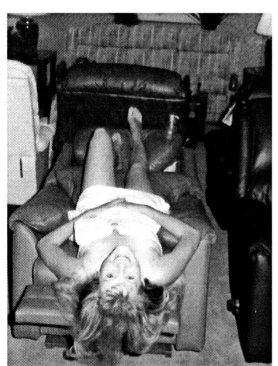

These were my all natural days. No changed hair color, no augmentation, just me!!

Always posing.

Chapter Three

After speaking to different people, I found that if I was not in print somewhere or had national exposure an article would not be done on me for poker. I had won a lot of money playing Texas Holdem. I actually bought almost all my jewelry, furniture, etc. from the game. I had done well in many tournaments around the local area—California and Nevada. I named my dog "Holdem" for the love and passion I have for the game. I realized this was, maybe, my edge.

I was one of the few successful Texas Holdem players in the United States and was known by hundreds of the top players in the business. I had never entered a huge tournament such as the World Championship of Poker that costs $10,000 to enter. These events get you lots of exposure if you win. I was professional enough to win money, but I was not a gambler. I knew it when I started playing years ago. Texas Holdem is one of the few casino games that are not played against the house. It is played directly against the players at the table. This is why you will not find many poker rooms in the large casinos in Vegas because they do not make enough profit. The house makes money by taking a drop (a little bit of money) for each hand played. You could lose hundreds of dollars and the house would not gain any more than the forced drop per hand. This is one reason that you will get hardly any comps in Vegas when playing because they really don't want you to play. Comps mean the casino, if you are a big gambler, lets you stay for free.

Anyhow, since I had not won a large event, or even entered one, for me to get noticed and be in one of the nationwide poker magazines I would need to win a large tournament. Or would I? I was playing poker at a local Casino in Arizona when I spoke to a guy sitting next to me. It was a fluke—or fate. He was from Vegas and was a known writer for *Poker Digest*. I batted my eyes, my mind spinning, and asked him to dinner at a nice restaurant in the casino. He had done the last cover of *Poker Digest*. Bruce accompanied me.

I made a proposal to the writer: "You need to write a story about me for the magazine. I'll pay you to write the story and if you can get it on the cover I'll give you a $500 bonus."

"Good idea, good material. I think I can make this work," he said.

Why not? I was a professional poker player, good looking, and well-known. I hadn't won a national title, but I was still a local champ. We e-mailed back and forth, and I wrote many pages for him to make his story.

Here is the unedited version of what I sent the writer of *Poker Digest*:

Jill Ann Spaulding, Age 30, Birth date 4-29-70, Bust 38 Waist 25 Hips 35, 118 pounds, 5'7", blue eyes, blonde hair, never married, only child. Never pregnant, I have an 8-pound toy poodle named Holdem after my favorite game. No tattoos and nothing pierced, not even my ears.

I was born in Phoenix, Arizona, and moved to Washington State when I was four and grew up in a very small town called Granite Falls. I lived there until I was fourteen years of age, and then our family moved back to Phoenix. My major interest in high school was retail marketing. I won a lot of trophies for Apparel and Accessories. I graduated from Mountain View High School in Mesa, Arizona, on the honor roll. I had a job at a donut shop. I was a tool girl at the swap meet and worked at Miller's Outpost my senior year. I moved out when I was eighteen. I had saved up enough for a large down payment on a mobile home and purchased my own mobile home for $31,500. My monthly payment was $333.38. Why at such a young age did I have so much money saved up? My father was a consistent influence in my life. Every conversation was about money. When I think back on my childhood, I remember my parents would fight about money. I vowed to never have this as one of the arguments in my life. This is why it was easy to save money. I wanted to move out! When my parents found out that I had saved up this much money, instead of being proud of me, they assumed I was having sex for money, selling drugs, or blackmailing someone. I guess I did not have a good rapport at home. I had actually saved the money not doing any of those things. By the age of eighteen, I had never been drunk, never smoked or taken anything illegal. The worst thing I ever did was to send a lot of Pizza Hut pizzas to a guy who broke up with me when I was seventeen.

My family was very happy to see me move out. I was a teenaged know-it-all. Actually my family did make a winner out of me. I had been drilled and lectured for so many years that I was determined to put what I knew to good use. My biggest motivation was that my mother was certain I would be back living at home in six months and would have lost my down payment. I didn't even have a job when I bought the trailer. I soon got a job working at Village Inn. I didn't make much on tips; the patrons were mostly coffee drinkers. I had worked my entire shift on Christmas day and when I was about to leave I was told that if I did not stay and work a double shift that they would be firing me. How little did they know if they would have just asked me I would have stayed. I decided to let myself go and took off my apron and walked out. I tried several different types of work, but nothing really clicked.

I loved to organize so I decided to start cleaning homes. I put an ad in the local paper, and before long I was doing nothing else. After one year I had over 100 employees and was no longer cleaning—but managing and training. Within two and a half years I had paid off my trailer. I owned it and the land free and clear.

Finally at the age of twenty-one, I went to a little country bar on Valentine's night. I went alone. As it happened, a man I had met a week earlier was there, alone as well. Bruce Gifford was forty-three (twenty-two years my senior). It never occurred to me that we would have anything permanent because of the age difference. He showed up at my door for a casual evening with roses and candy. I was hooked. My family was not. They threatened to disown me. My father threatened to kill him. We didn't speak for almost five years. Not just because of Bruce—there were other issues as well. Now my mom and I talk a couple of times a year. My father and I do not have a relationship anymore. Bruce and I have been together the entire time.

I admit he is the father figure I longed for because my dad and I were never close even when I was a toddler. We never did marry because of Bruce's family's reaction and my family's reaction. At this point we probably never will. For anyone curious, his wife was involved with another man before I ever met Bruce, and she is married to this guy till this day. This will hopefully stop any questions. As for me being with him for his money, he did not have any money at all. He only had his job and the clothes on his back. He was left with virtually nothing. He came out of the entire relationship with no house, no vehicle. The only thing that he was left with was ½ of his retirement, which was $15,000. He is my best friend, and I feel this is why the relationship works.

Taking a few steps back, I opened a new and recycled clothing store. Why? I was ridiculed when I went to school for not having all the name brands. I named the store *Name Brand Exchange*. It fit. One day I woke up and took stock of my life. The trailer was paid off, and I decided I didn't want to deal with the employees in my cleaning business anymore. It took about six months to get up the inventory to open my new store. It was an exciting time—and still is. I love it. Not every day did I love it, though. I got so stressed out from employees stealing, quitting, or me having to fire them for ridiculous things. I was at my wit's end. I had moved into a new house and had it paid off in two years. I paid $125,000 for it so it wasn't so easy to close the doors or sell the business that was making good money. I went to a doctor for the stress. He advised me to double the employees' pay and don't go back. That was three years ago, and I have held true to my commitment. I don't make as much money, but my employees are well-paid, they don't quit, and I don't have to see the place. I still make a comfortable living and can play poker every day of the week. Life is great. My passion is going to the movies. That is my other hobby. I can get completely immersed in a movie and take myself away.

I live in a large house now. It was paid off until recently when I purchased two commercial pads to build a small 8,000 square foot strip mall. I'm in debt again. I will be putting my store in about 3,800 square feet and renting out the rest, planning to use this for my retirement. I still work out three times a week with weights and riding my bike. My favorite shows are *Ally McBeal* and *Sex and the City*.

Chapter Four

Why poker—and how did I get started? When Harrah's first opened in Arizona, Bruce and I went out there to play slots. They had an instructional table of seven-card stud for free, fake money, and I talked Bruce into sitting down. We learned how to play right then and there. I was not hooked yet. Marques, the instruction table guy, told me what to play and convinced me to enter a tournament to get some cheap, free practice. I entered the tournament and got second place—around $800. I was hooked. I've been playing ever since.

Why do I love poker? To me, it's like a great big party that doesn't end until you want it to. You can come and play any time you want, day or night, and you will always recognize many of the players and most of the dealers. Over the years, all these people have become friends. Most people know me by my first name. I am known all over the world because of poker. I have many friends in Europe, Australia, Canada, France, and many other countries—all thanks to poker. I love the sensation of my heart in a flutter when I get a great hand. I love the adrenalin from check-raising, re-raising, folding, and bluffing. It is an incredible drug I cannot get enough of—but I am sensible enough to know when to stop. I know all of the world champions and have played against most of them in poker tournaments on my same table. I consider myself a professional poker player because when I tally my wins against my losses, I'm in the black. My favorite casino is any one that has a Holdem game. I have played in hundreds of tournaments. Mostly small and, of course, I try to play the ones where the casino puts up the cash. Women should love playing poker. Their husbands or boyfriends could stay playing longer—which they would love—and since there are not as many women poker players we do get all of the attention. Everyone is so nice to me.

Why with the exciting life of a gambler, did I want to pose for *Playboy* magazine? Believe it or not, I was brought up to be very liberal and to take care of my man. This is what my mother taught me and I'm sticking to it. Keep him tired, and he won't cheat. Let him look. What's the harm? So I tried to follow the rules of plenty of water, sex, and food—the basic necessities. If you tell men they cannot look, they will look more. So what did I do? I ordered *Playboy* television and *Playboy* magazine. I took him to any strip bar that he wanted to see. This way I wouldn't wonder what he was doing there. I got to see it up close.

Why pose for *Playboy*? I just guess I wanted to prove to Bruce and myself that I was just as pretty as those girls in those magazines. I really also wanted to go to the *Playboy* mansion and go to some of those crazy parties. They looked like so much fun! I guess I just wanted to glimpse the world I had seen in the pages of a magazine—see a fantasy come to life. I always felt I was the girl next door type that *Playboy* is famous for. I am very honest, down to earth, and feel that everyone has something good inside.

Back to poker, being a woman playing poker has its difficulties. It seems especially that, with blonde hair, no one figures I know how to play. Bluffing is sometimes impossible with many of the gentlemen because they always assume that I don't know what I have or that I don't have anything. In turn, I will then have to play very conservatively because they will call me down. I will need to have the best hand, but again, they will drop because I have to play so conservatively they will know I have a hand. This relates to the good players, of course.

The comical thing about being a woman playing poker is that some men are such gentlemen that they will not raise me or even bet. I will think I have a good hand and keep betting, then they turn over this monstrous hand. I was the one betting . . . they were nicely checking as gentlemen. Oops. This is confusing. When men check (which means they are not trying to "raise" me) I think they are weak and I will bet, but a lot of times they are strong and just being nice to the "little lady." So, the button advantage is different for me because of this. I don't mind. I love everything about poker, and I understand that many of the men don't like a woman playing poker. They feel it's a man's game. I'm just glad to be a part of the action and am having the time of my life. And, as you can see . . . I am no "dumb blonde." I have to think through all the various possibilities at the table in order to win the way I do.

*   *   *   *   *   *

Favorite Color: Black
Favorite Car: White BMW – but I will probably never own one as I cannot see spending that kind of money on a vehicle to get me from point A to point B.

Favorite Animal: My poodle named Holdem. She is a girl's best friend and the smartest dog. She knows when I'm busy and don't want to play and follows me everywhere I go.

Favorite Stuffed Toy: Teddy Bear

Favorite Movie: *Titanic.* I felt this movie in my heart for days after seeing it.

Favorite Person: Shirley Temple. As my all-time favorite actress she embodies my admiration for her ability to help many people during the Depression with that classic smile. She helped me get through many of the difficult times in my life, and I had many pictures of her in my room since I was ten.

*   *   *   *   *

I planned to play in the World Series of Poker and the Tournament of Champions (TOC). I had not entered one of these large events yet. I had been preparing in the smaller tournaments to make sure I was ready.

I decided that if I was going to make the cover that the picture would have to be terrific. It would have to be so good that they would want it to be on the cover. I also decided that if I was going to submit my pictures to *Playboy* that I would want them as great as they could be, not from my own personal camera with whatever lighting was in the room. I decided that this was the perfect opportunity to do both at the same time—a hopeful picture for *Poker Digest* and a great nude for *Playboy*. I decided to stage my own photo shoot. Again, I am the type of person who believes you can take control of your own destiny. I called my makeup artist who had helped me to learn how to improve my skills and told her that I needed to do a full photo shoot for the cover of *Poker Digest* and a few nudes to send to *Playboy*. She recommended a photographer, and we discussed all the plans for the shots and the pricing, which was huge! We did the photo shoot at my house.

I had explained the goal. I had the perfect purple card table and props, and we did another shot with me and some cards that never got used. We also did the shot that I was planning to send to *Playboy*. If you can imagine this, I had every centerfold I ever loved opened out on top of the pool table for basic help with how to stand, what *Playboy* prefers pictures to look like, etc. I had every high-heeled pair of shoes I owned for the shoot. Both the photographer and Bruce decided the shoe selection. This was the second time ever in my life to pose nude. It was very exciting. The makeup artist spent about an hour working on me. The photographer seemed inexperienced and unprofessional, however. I had the vision that I wanted, but it just wasn't going to happen with this guy. He gave me all the rolls of film and told me the best place to have them developed. When I got them back they were mostly dark, without light, it was a waste.

Suzi Simpson wrote back on 1-31-01:

Hi Jill!
I just found this e-mail. So sorry I didn't get to you sooner. I get over 600 e-mails a day . . . a bit overwhelming. Anyways I hope they loved you! I've seen them reject goddesses and wonder to myself how I ever made it. I'd be happy to put you on my site if that would help you get traffic back to yours!

I responded on 2-2-01:

Dear Suzi,
I got turned down. I got my regret letter about a week later. I really felt that I had a chance since the photographer said that they would be calling me the next day or first thing the following Monday. Then when Wednesday came and no one had called I spoke to the lady who writes the regret letters and said that she did not understand why the photographer said this, that they contact everyone by mail and it would be about two weeks, and then the following week I got the letter from her saying no. I have not given up though, I just had some other pictures taken and I am going to send them in again. This is what she suggested doing; just keep sending them in, so I am. That is so nice of you to offer to put me on your site; I will think about this. I don't have a site at all, but if I get one, I will sure take you up on it. I will put you on my site also. I will write and tell you the latest news. Thanks for all of your support. I really want to just some day go to the *Playboy* mansion, I just have dreamed about it, and this is the main reason that I wanted to pose—just to go. I want to see the grounds, the mansion, the exotic animals, and just what goes on there. I went to bid on being able to go to the mansion on Playboyauction.com but it goes for $10,000 almost every time! This is what gave me the idea to pose and I thought that maybe I wouldn't have to pay the $10,000. I want to go before I get married because I probably won't be allowed to go after I'm married.
Well, lots of love and luck.

About a month later, she responded on 3-1-01:

Hi Jill!
There's an event coming up in April called "Road to the Playboy Mansion." Check it out because if you know any corporate people it's a tax write-off and you could be their "Hot Date." I'm going to be there working, and it should be one heck of a party. It's impossible to get in anymore, but this could be a good way and if Hef saw you maybe he'd pick you to be a centerfold. You're pretty, don't give up! Suzi

I didn't go to the event, but it was nice that she thought of me. Again, I was fooled . . . I thought everyone would be like Suzi. I thought there was a "sisterhood" of Playmates.

I sent a few of the pictures that I liked best and the story to the writer for Poker Digest. *He submitted the story and the edgy, sexy profile on me was a hit. The writer did get many of the facts incorrect all the way down to stating my dog's name was Aces. Who knows how he dreamed up this name, as my dog's name has always been Holdem. The magazine was perfect. I had made the cover, and to top it off, the biggest two weeks in poker—Binion's World Series of Poker, where every champion from far and wide attended—and there was my picture on the cover. When I went to Binion's, not only did I sign autographs and take pictures with everyone, I was a semi-celebrity. It was terrific. The magazine came out April 20 – May 3, 2001 Vol. 4/No. 9 $2.95. I was on the top of a purple card table and the cover read "Poker's Wonder Girl Jill Ann Spaulding: Advantages and Disadvantages of being a Female Poker Player." It was a four-page article with full color pictures. It was just what I needed. I was so excited to try again. Loaded with my* Poker Digest *magazine and my nude photos taken from the same photo shoot, I was ready to send my submission to Playboy. I contacted the writer from* Poker Digest *and told him I was ready for him to write the letter for me to Playboy. We e-mailed back and forth and came up with the following:*

I just discovered a poker player who wins major tournaments—and she's gorgeous!
You're probably aware that poker is the most popular card game in America, and its appeal is growing internationally, as is evidenced by the growing number of poker tournaments in England, Australia, Germany, France, and the Caribbean. Although more men than women enjoy the game, its appeal is spreading to the fairer sex.

Jill Ann Spaulding is a stunning blonde whose measurements are 38–24–35 and are proof of the game's popularity.

The enclosed article and photos speak for themselves. Jill Ann is a very unusual woman who would, I feel, make a welcome contribution to your magazine.

1. She has an incredible body and has cover girl good looks. The editors of POKER DIGEST felt that was the case, and I hope you agree.
2. She works out regularly to keep in shape.
3. By age eighteen, she had saved enough money to buy her own home and launched a successful business
4. She began playing poker and got so good at it she became a professional, traveling many months out of the year playing in major poker tournaments. Her ambition: to win the World Series of Poker. She knows poker players all over the world, and is acquainted with many poker legends including Amarillo Slim Preston, Puggy Pearson, Oklahoma Johnny Hale, John Bonetti, Tom McEvoy, Johnny Chan, T.J. Cloutier and Phil Hellmuth, who, at twenty-four, became the youngest person to ever win the World Series of Poker.

Would *Playboy* be interested in doing a photo article on Spaulding? I believe your readers would be interested in her philosophy that older men make better lovers. Her skill in a male-dominated game and a disciplined training program that has given her a perfectly proportioned body would also appeal to *Playboy* readers. I am a journalist and magazine writer with some 2,400 articles published in *PEOPLE WEEKLY* (I served as Arizona correspondent for eight years), *WESTERN HORSEMAN, FORD TIME, SKI MAGAZINE, TV TIME*, and *ALASKAN AIRWAYS, HUSTLER, THE STAR, ENQUIRER, SEX OLOGY* and many other publications.

If you are interest in pursuing the project you can call me at XXX-XXXX or e-mail me at *xxx@xxx.com*. I would appreciate the return of the enclosed photos when you are finished with them. Thank you for your consideration.

Sincerely,
Geno Lawrenzi
Director of Marketing-Publicity

I received two regret letters. I sent the above letter to the Chicago office and also to the Santa Monica office. The letters were almost the same as the one I got from the first Playmate test. Basically, they reminded me how fierce the competition was . . . and I was just not quite right.

I waited about three months of the same year around July or August and sent them again and received the same response.

I resubmitted them again the first of February and received a very similar response thanking me for submitting . . . but no.

Well, with all of the surgeries, the frustration, the pain, the work-outs, the let-down, I decided to submit my pictures to www.Playboy.com. I had only submitted to Playboy for Playmate or for an inside article in the magazine. I really did not want to do Playboy.com. I wanted so badly to be in the magazine, but at this point I was willing to do the online thing. It was the year 2000 when I started this venture, and now it was 2002! Not that I knew I would be chosen, but looking at the competition, I felt that it was a much easier option based on four girls online a month, and overall fifty-two girls a year—instead of twelve for the entire year for the magazine. (Hey, as a poker player, I know all about the odds, and my chances online were better!) I had this article that I had printed out from many months prior so I decided to submit my Poker Digest *magazine, the following letter and three pictures of me nude.*

ACTUAL AD THAT WAS ON THE PLAYBOY WEBSITE:
MODEL SEARCH

Playboy.com is looking for women 18 and older for upcoming pictorials, features and other modeling opportunities. Please send photos – preferably a full body shot and a headshot – in any format, demonstrating your finest features and a clear copy of a photo ID that shows date of birth. Send them to Jill Norton, Photo Editor, Playboy Online, 680 N. Lake Shore Drive, 14th Floor, Chicago, Il 60611. While nudity is not required, it is preferred. Please include any information about yourself that may be interesting to us. Selected candidates will be brought in to our Chicago offices to be tested by a Playboy.com photographer.

I sent my letter to Jill Norton and called about a week later to follow up to see if she had received my pictures, letter, and magazine only to find out that she was no longer with the company. They gave me two different names that had taken over her department: John Thomas and Chad Doering. I immediately made two new packages with my pictures, letter, and magazine for these two gentlemen. I sent the packages certified mail, return receipt requested, on February 6, 2002.

Dear (Jill Norton, John Thomas, and Chad Doering):
  I would love to become a cyber Playboy.com girl. I am 5'7' blonde hair, blue eyes, 118 pounds 38-24-35. What makes me unique is that I am Poker's Wonder Girl. I am one of the most famous women poker players and I was recently (April 2001) put on the cover of *Poker Digest*, a nationwide magazine, with a full-page story about my life. I know that I am thirty-one and it is probably over your age limit, but many of the most beautiful photographed women in the world are around my age (Jennifer Lopez 31, Lucy Liu 33, Faith Hill 34, Nicole Kidman 34, Ashley Judd 33, Mariah Carey 32, Gwyneth Paltrow 29, Sarah Jessica Parker 36, Julia Roberts 34, Cameron Diaz 29). A recent playmate was twenty-nine (Tina Marie Jordan). Please make an exception. I am willing to travel at my expense, take off whatever time is necessary for events.

The same day I sent the letters to Playboy.com, I sent a letter to Hugh Hefner with just one nude photo and the following:

Dear Hef:
  I would love to be invited to one of your parties. I am single, 5'7" with blonde hair, blue eyes, 118 pounds 38-24-35. What makes me unique is that I am Poker Digest's Wonder Girl. I am one of the most famous women poker players, and I was featured on the cover of April 2001 *Poker Digest*, a nationwide magazine with a full-page story about my life.
  With love,
  Jill Ann Spaulding.

It finally happened. I remember the call. I was upstairs in my office when the phone rang, and Chad Doering was on the line saying that they would like to do a special on me about my poker skills, and he told me it paid $750 for the day and that they would be flying me to Chicago to do the shoot. They would take care of all the expenses.
  I was so excited, but tried to stay calm. I had a totally positive attitude. I said, "Let's do it." Chad said it would be in about two to three weeks. I took his number and thanked him. I went out into the hallway and started scream-

ing! "Guess who called! Guess who called!" I shouted to Bruce. He could not guess. I said, "*Playboy*! They want me for a shoot in two to three weeks in Chicago!"

Bruce gave me a great big hug and said that I deserved it. I had worked so hard and kept at it, and he was so proud of me. Of course, there was no real celebrating—the working out and diet were on! I had been slacking because I had basically given up. I called Trent Clark, my trainer, and told him the news and he started coming over two to four times a week all the way up to the shoot to get me prepared. He mapped out a diet plan for me (not losing weight, but building muscle by increasing protein). I could eat whatever I wanted as long as it was on the list Trent gave me.

It was a long weekend, and I was excited about Chad Doering calling me back. This happened to be the same time we were going to Vegas with Bruce's parents. We drove to Vegas Sunday; no one called on Monday. Tuesday came and I had just gone into the restroom and handed the phone to Bruce, and Chad called asking for Joan, Bruce said sorry no Joan. They both hung up. A few minutes later the phone rang again, and Chad asked for Joan again. Bruce said, "No Joan. Maybe you mean Jill Ann?"

"That's it . . . sorry," Chad said. Bruce put me on the phone. Chad apologized for calling me by the wrong name; he told me my shoot was scheduled for 3/4/02 to 3/5/02.

"Is that okay, Jill Ann?"

Of course, even if I had to reschedule something it would have been okay! Chad said he would call me back with the flight times. About two hours later, we were in our hotel room, and Chad called and I wrote down all of the times etc. After we hung up, I was so excited. I called my grandma and told her right away. She was very excited for me. I finished the trip to Vegas on cloud nine (of course, I did stick to my diet the entire trip!). When we finally got back, I called Chad and finalized a few things (how to do my nails, hair, bikini line, etc.) About four days later, Penny Ekkert called and told me that Chad would be gone for awhile and she was taking over. I was suddenly terrified; I figured he got fired and now, after I had already been through a couple of disappointments, I might not get chosen because of the change in personnel. Everything that Chad had told me was slightly different from what Penny Ekkert told me. I was so confused. Chad told me no bikini line, Penny told me that I must have a bikini line because completely bare in the pubic area was too revealing for *Playboy*. At the time, I had no hair so I knew I had to grow it back right away. They told me short, natural-looking nails (and color clear). About four days before the shoot was to happen, I still did not have plane tickets, or information on where I was staying. I was very concerned that it would be canceled at any time. Finally the packet came from Penny Ekkert.

I was glad and finally asked her what had happened to Chad.

"Did he quit or get fired?"

"Who told you that," she asked

I said no one. The real story was Peggy said she had no way of calling or contacting him before my shoot. This didn't sound good. She then said Chad was actually photographing Miss Cyber Girl of the Year in some exotic Mexican locale. I was so relieved Chad wasn't gone. I ate correctly and exercised for the two and a half weeks prior to the shoot. I started to believe that this was finally coming true.

Believe it or not, while I was preparing for my shoot, Hugh Hefner himself wrote back:

February 27, 2002
Dear Jill:
With that impressive nude photo, I feel obliged to put you on our party list. See you soon.
Love, Hef
Hugh M. Hefner
HMH/dr

I was amazed. It was as if all these dreams in my life were coming true at the same time.

To get ready for the shoot, I had Jenny at Ulta Source color my roots. I had Connie do my eyebrows, lip, and chin. I had a lady named Claudia do my bikini line, underarms and a facial. I had my nails done and used Perfect Tan for that sun-blushed look. I was set and boarded the plane.

After the flight, I went down the escalators to find a large sign saying "Jill Spaulding." The man holding the sign called for them to bring the car around. The driver offered me any of several beverages; I accepted water. I called Bruce and my grandparents to let them know I had arrived safely. The driver let me out at the front door of the hotel, and I checked in.

Believe it or not, to give you some idea of how sheltered I was in many ways, I asked one of the front desk gentlemen to walk me to the room. I was scared. I had not stayed in a hotel alone or anywhere alone and was a little worried about my safety. The young man walked me to my room. I pushed a chair up to the door so that the door could not be opened and felt much safer. I let my family know that I was locked safely in the room. It was already 11:00 p.m., and I needed to get sleep, but I also had to have my legs and body freshly-shaved for the mornings shoot. I had to use little water as to not remove my tan, but be careful to make sure I did not cut myself in any place. Overwhelmed by the event, my eyes were bloodshot. They looked awful. I think the anticipation and a mixture of fear took over me, and I had not slept well in a few nights. Thank goodness for eye drops.

That night, I did not sleep well, and the hotel did not give me the wake-up call that I had asked for. Luckily my grandma and Bruce both made sure to call me at the time I was to wake up. I ate a banana that I had brought with me and grabbed another one when leaving the hotel.

Next I took a cab to *Playboy* Headquarters. The driver seemed to know exactly where it was. My heels clicked on the marble floors as I made my way to the appointed floor, my heart beating rapidly. The receptionist on the 15th floor was very nice, and after I gave her my name she said someone would be with me shortly.

"You must be the poker girl."

"Yes, I am," I replied.

"I've seen your set. It looks very cool."

We chatted for a little while. I had to sit there without any makeup while the entire crew from *Playboy* entered to go into their desk areas. Ordinarily, I wouldn't mind (as I said, I used to wear very little makeup), but here at *Playboy* headquarters, I knew some of the most beautiful and sexy women in the world—household names!—walked through those doors. The reception-ist offered me *Playboy* magazines to take home, but I already had those. I showed her my pictures of my *Playboy* poolroom with the eight-foot by eight-foot bunny on the wall and all the autographed pictures. She was very en-thused about them.

At about 9:15, they took me to the studio where the makeup artist was waiting for me. She was very nice.

"Take all your clothes off and put on the robe hanging there. I'll be back shortly."

She took me to another dressing room and showed me some outfits that she had picked out that she thought I would look great in. They were mostly gold. I never wore gold and couldn't imagine why it would look good on me now. She was persistent on a particular one, and I tried to trust her expertise. We returned to the makeup station, and she put hot rollers in my hair. As soon as she was done, she started on the makeup. The photographer came down and introduced himself as George Georgiou. Then Chad introduced himself—he popped in and out of the shoot from time to time, though he mainly shot things on location.

It seemed like hardly any time had passed, and I was ready. Gold stretch pants, G-string underwear, a bustier with little pantyhose that attached an additional bra, a gold shirt, belt, bracelet, necklace, and earrings. To me, it was not flattering and the gold stretch pants were double my size. Finally, they were ready for me out on the set. It was very cute with a velvet-looking red background. Everyone introduced himself or herself. Pat, the makeup artist/stylist/wardrobe, stayed on the set the entire time. Brynne Rinderknecht was the set coordinator. George Georgious was the photographer, and David Goodman was his light man. Chad came down a few times to check on how it was going. The shoot area was very dark, which made me feel very comfortable. It was seductive somehow, intimate. The photographer showed me where to stand and what poses they would like. Before each roll of film they took a Polaroid to check the lighting. They showed me the pose and then would tell me for each picture to just slightly move my head, mouth, and arms to make each picture slightly different. They told me to undress slowly. The photographer would tell me the pose, come up and help me achieve it. This went on for nineteen rolls of film. I felt very confident. I was in good shape, and I felt I looked like a real *Playmate*, and that confidence made this whole experience much easier. The confidence showed through.

We broke for lunch, and I still had not even bared my stomach. I had brought my letter from Hef with me to Chicago, thinking they would somehow be nicer to me knowing that Hef approved of me and was inviting me to his party. It didn't go over well at all. Most of them had worked for *Playboy* for a long time and never had been invited to the mansion. The few times that they had gone it was only for work, and they were forced to leave before the festivities started. Suddenly I felt out of place and uncomfortable following their reaction. They got into a huge discussion about it and were very upset. I couldn't understand what the problem was, but apparently I was it. Instead of being impressed by my invitation, they were quite petty, accusing me of using them. Worse, nothing could have been further from the truth! I don't live my life that way.

Lunch ended, and Pat touched up my makeup. We finished the rest of the shoot. Then they had me put on a red shirt and hat because I was to sign both of them and they were going to auction them off on the internet for my fans. My fans! I felt like I was embarking on a new life. My handwriting didn't look very good, but I signed them anyway. It was exciting just getting to sign something. Then the light guy told me that the pictures were done.

"Do you want to see them?"

"Absolutely!" I followed him into the photography room.

A lady in there got really angry that I was in there. The photographer was quickly reviewing the negatives with an eyeglass. I looked only for a second and returned to the lunch area of the studio. A freshly polished Town Car with leather seats was waiting to take me to the airport. While waiting to board I still had a lot of makeup on and people were staring at me. I was wearing an "I Love Playboy" shirt! Two people asked if I was a *Playboy* girl. I said I was and gave out two autographs. It was fun. I even had some guy who was traveling on the same flight take a picture of me so I could remember what I looked like.

I was instructed that I needed to write an article for my Playboy.com pictorial about Texas Holdem. I ended up getting a writer who unfortunately had no concept at all about how to play the game. I guess, because I am a naturally good player and have done so well with it that I didn't realize how complex the game was until I had to explain it to someone who had no knowledge of it. I realized how much experience I had throughout the years and that I was a very educated Texas Holdem player. I put together an initial article for Blair R. Fischer, closing with:

"...I could write a huge book. There are so many details of each one of the ideas I have presented here. I just tried to keep it simple—similar to the pool and tennis article so not to overwhelm the readers who are not advanced Holdem players. If more detail is needed or wanted I can provide a million different small or large details of this very exciting and fast-paced game..."

Blair responded weeks after I had e-mailed him, saying that my draft was too focused and he needed something more for the layperson, the guy who knew nothing about poker. The article needed to be more general. This is the second draft I wrote —friendly and easy:

I.   "Hi guys. I am a professional poker player, but I am going to teach you how to have a great time, win money and not have to know all of the ins and outs of poker. When I go to Vegas, I like the free drinks and the fun of chatting with everyone at the table. This makes it very hard to be a great player. Mix alcohol and talking and you are not paying attention; you are easy pickings for the professional poker player. When I am in this mood—just there to have a good time, let loose, flirt and joke—I do the following: *Don't play too many hands. Just play large pocket pairs and large suited connectors (Ace and King in the same suit, King and Queen in the same suit, etc.). Enjoy the conversation, the free drinks, and the great time of playing poker. If you follow my hand selection guide you will not only have a great time, you will also be a winner at the game.*

2.   The higher the limit the more advanced the players get, stick to the smaller games and there will be more weekend warriors out to have a good time. They are less serious, you won't win as much, but you can't lose as much either and, with the professional skills of the advanced players, stick to the lower limits.

3.   Making friends at the poker table is going to always happen. I have the problem with talking with everyone and then I don't want to take his or her money. On nights that you are out to have a good time, that's fine. If you are really serious about winning and being a pro, no talking, no drinking, no fun—all business.

4.   Know your players. Just because they are blonde and blue-eyed does not mean they haven't been playing for a long time. Know which players you can bluff, raise, or just know when you need to get out of the hand. Categorize your players when you sit down at the table. This will make it easier for you to know who to call, bluff, or raise.

a.   Conservative: You can easily make this player lay down a better hand than you have because he may think you have him beat and the extra money of a check raise or re-raise will often make him fold.

b.   Weekend Warriors: This player is here to play. They have worked all week and no matter what you can bet they are not getting out—this is not a player to bluff.

c.   Pro: He knows you are capable of bluffing so he is going to figure you out. Bluffing works on a now and then basis with this player. Raising and check raising can only work if they are trying to make a move on you.

5. *Why play poker? It is a game where you have the advantage against the house (the casino). You are actually playing the players at the table, not the casino. The house does take a drop, but it is very minimal compared to slots and other table games. You can actually win consecutively at poker. It is not so much a game of chance like a slot machine. You decide your own destiny by what hands you choose to play.*

Blair's response to this was way too friendly and said he'd like to interview me over the phone and try to get the story that way.

When he called me his first question was "If you have a pair, when do you split the pair up and go for a straight or flush?"

"Blair, this is not draw poker." I had to start at ground zero and try to explain to him the entire game. It was very difficult. I realized then how much I had progressed from an intermediate Holdem player to have slang terms like fold, muck, river, turn, and flop. He had never heard them and was very confused. I realized right then how difficult the game was and how much I really knew.

* * * *

About this time, I had received that first letter from Hef and remembered that his birthday party was coming up. Based on Hef's letter I was expecting to get an invitation. Bruce said that Hef's staff probably didn't get a chance to put me on the party list, and I would probably get on the next one. He thought that the party list had been made long before I wrote. I looked back at Hef's letter and thought it really seemed as though he was excited to have me come and that there was plenty of time to have me put on the list—changes to which only he can make. I waited, hoping to receive an invitation, without success. I decided to write another letter. Thank goodness I did.

Dear Hef,
I can't believe you took the time to write back personally. It was a complete shock! I will keep this letter forever. Thank you so much. I so hope that I get invited to your birthday party so that I can wish you Happy Birthday in person, but if you have other plans for me, I will understand. I have been excited to check my mail every day since your letter arrived.
P.S. My photo shoot for Playboy.com is going to be published April 11, 2002. It is going to be under Guy 101 Poker. I teach the guys how to play Texas Holdem—my best game!

A few days later the Playboy Mansion called, telling me I was on the party list. They informed me of the time, date, and dress code. I was so excited.
The following letter was sent to my friends and family about me getting to go to the Playboy Mansion for Hugh Hefner's birthday bash.

I am writing a letter to all of you so you can read about my adventure to the Playboy Mansion on April 6, 2002 Hugh Hefner's 76th birthday. To prepare, I had a guy named Jeremy do my hair at 2:15 and Zethina do my makeup at 3:00 at a salon in Scottsdale. From there Bruce and I went to the airport and took a flight out at 5:30 pm to LAX. Commerce Casino, the hotel where we were staying for the night, sent a van to pick us up. We checked in and then went downstairs to get a floor man to see if they would authorize dropping me off at the *Playboy* Mansion. Luckily, they recognized me and I had called prior asking for it. It was written on a piece of paper that I would be going. So, at 8:30 the hotel provided us a free limo to UCLA where the pick-up point was for the party. The driver did not know where UCLA was! We had the letter with me from Mr. Hefner and his home address so we went to the mansion, but they would not allow the driver to drop us off there. We had to make our way to UCLA. The door person at the mansion told the driver how to get there, but he didn't listen and we were lost again. A half-hour trip turned into about 1 hour and 15 minutes.

We got to the destination point at UCLA and then came the big scare—was my name on the list? There was also a huge sign that read NO PERSONAL CAMERAS, so I took my camera out of my purse and gave it to Bruce. The driver and Bruce waited for me to make sure before leaving me there. There were lots of people. They had the alphabet divided up in threes and everyone stood in the line their last name corresponded with. When it was my turn, to my delight, my name was there. I had to show two forms of ID to prove my identity. They stamped my left hand with some kind of stamp. I gave the shuttle driver and Bruce the thumbs up and they drove off.

A man with a Polaroid gave me a number to remember and snapped a picture. He wrote my cell number down and then put my picture with that corresponding number. This way they could decide if they would invite you back to the next party or not, based on looks or whatever. We all piled into an elevator and at the top we got into a shuttle bus that took us to the mansion less than a mile away. They indicated that there was not enough parking for everyone to drive their own vehicles. The only people allowed to park at the mansion were the stars or close friends.

We entered the gates of the mansion, and it was so beautiful; the entire pathway was lit up with tiny white Christmas lights. When we stopped at the front door and we all got out, they checked each hand for the proper stamp. Through the door there was a coat and purse valet. I chose not to but the lady suggested I look around first and then decide. I had seen a line of girls when I first walked in and took my place there. It was a line for a one-stall bathroom. All of us wanted to check our appearance.

It didn't take long, but while I was in line I asked a girl next to me if this was the only bathroom. She replied "Aren't you a Playmate? You should know."

At that point I was in great spirits; felt I really fit in. I could tell right away that almost everyone knew each other and that most of them had come with two or three of their girlfriends. All of the guests seemed to be from California and live pretty close to the mansion. I felt a little nervous, too. Like high school all over again. I decided to walk around—see who was there. The dance floor was right near the entrance, and I made my way through the people dancing and found a room filled with desserts—chocolate-covered strawberries, cookies, chocolates and fresh strawberries. I asked two very cute, very young waiters if it was alright to be in there. They told me that anywhere was okay. Off of this room there was another with tables with older people drinking. None of them were in lingerie. I passed an open bar where there were many people in line for drinks and a full complement of bartenders serving.

I wandered down some steps and there, to the right, was Hugh Hefner and all of his girlfriends. My heart stopped. Suddenly I heard my name called. I turned around to see the photographer from Chicago who had picked me for the shoot. I was so excited to see him. He was the first person I had seen that I knew. He was pleased for me that I had gotten an invitation to the party. He told me to go over to Hef, and he would take my picture and e-mail it to me. So I scooted over to Hef and asked if I could take a picture with him. He stood up and we posed. Then I went right back to Chad. He showed me what it looked like on his digital camera. I thanked him, and he wished me a good evening. I was off again.

I passed another open bar. I headed to the pool area where there was yet another large open bar. I wandered down another hallway where I found a sauna, steam room, and about three bathroom areas with styling stations. No one was in the pool, but there were a lot of people sitting around it. There were electric heaters everywhere to keep guests warm. Finally, I hooked up with this beautiful girl name Rhonda. She was a clothing designer, and she happened to make clothes for one of Hefner's girls. We hit it off and hung out the entire night until about 2:30 a.m. when she went home. We toured the place, doing nothing in particular. She was there with two other girls and knew everyone. I followed them as they made the rounds. I was in line waiting to go to the bathroom again and this friend of Rhonda's asked what month I was. I told them that this month I was on Playboy.com and that it was my first time at a party; that I had come by myself. They invited me to join them, but I told them I was already forcing Rhonda to take me with her. They laughed and said if I changed my mind I could hang out with them. The rest of the night they waved and said hello as they passed by.

Rhonda started talking to this guy for a long time in one of the sauna rooms so I hung out with some other girls that we had been dancing with. The group was Miss June and her three friends. The party was awesome, and I never felt that anyone was staring at me. The stars were busy talking to whoever was trying to get their attention at the time. Otherwise there was no one kissing or having sex.

It was a fantastic party. The ratio was about 1 guy for every 10 gals. They had two large areas with food that included gigantic shrimp, fruit, and finger sandwiches. There were no speeches, birthday wishes—nothing. I tried to sit down at the Hugh Hefner table with all of the girls. This did not work. I asked Amber, one of his most beautiful girlfriends, about it and she said the table was only for the current Playmates and his girlfriends. I told her I thought I would ask because many of the girls at the table were not as beautiful as his girlfriends so I thought it would be that anyone could sit down. She smiled and said that was so nice. As I walked away she repeated what I had said to Mr. Hefner, and he chuckled about it. I was being truthful. The table was set for about 15 and, at the time I asked, there were about 4 seats open. Can't say I didn't try.

I'm sure you're all wondering if I saw any celebrities. There were a lot of stars there, but I am not the best with names. Many of them I will not even list. I recognized them but could not remember their names. The ones I definitely knew were Weird Al, Keifer Sutherland, Scott Baio, Jeanette Jonsson, Jon Lovitz, Snoop Dog and his entire crew, Melissa Rivers, Stephanie Heinrich, Michelle Rodgers, Michael Bay (this is mentioned right below also), Matthew Perry and David Schwimmer from the TV sitcom "Friends" and Hef's brother. Drew Barrymore was reportedly there, but I didn't see her—what a shame!

In addition to all these famous people I also saw Playmate Ava Fabian and Mickey Rourke. Bush frontman, Gavin Rossdale, and video director, Shawn Mortensen, were flanked by the Van Patten brothers, Jimmy and Nels. *Pearl Harbor* director, Michael Bay and his girlfriend, Playmate Lisa Dergan, wished Hef a happy birthday. I saw, Kato Kalin, Judd Nelson, Kylie Bax, and *North by Northwest's* Martin Landau. All of the stars gave me hugs, even the guys. What a rush. They were regular people and seemed excited and very receptive to us talking with them.

I decided to look around the property. I went into the Grotto, which is the secret place at the mansion that everyone talks about. It was an incredible setting surrounded with plants, flowers—orchids in every color and blooming jasmine—and huge granite rocks. Even here, no detail was overlooked, and it had 10 huge candles burning to give it atmosphere. It was very humid because it was a size of four or five Jacuzzis all in one room. If you went under-water you could swim out into the pool. There were just a few couples sitting next to each area. There were girls with painted outfits on passing out Jell-o shooters. They were doing this for most of the night until they finally got to join the rest of the party. Though they were wearing nothing but paint it still covered more than a lot of the other people were wearing.

Everyone was taking pictures, and I could have had the best collection of shots if I hadn't followed the rules and left the camera behind. I could have taken rolls and rolls. Everything was so amazing. I know I'll never forget it, but it would have been wonderful to have the pictures. There were two bare-breasted girls wearing g-strings and jewels on their nipples. Otherwise, it was very tame. No one was wearing anything overly revealing—no more so than you would see in an L.A. or Manhattan club. I would say that the bathing suits I see at a local beach were more revealing. I didn't see anyone flash anyone. I did—twice—one for the movie camera guy when he was filming and one when they took a group picture with me, Hef and his girls. I figured this would be the only way I would make the *Playboy* mansion party video by doing it. So I did. We shall see. I rented the Playboy mansion party video before going to the party, and it seemed the only girls that were featured flashed or were very skimpily dressed. That's why I did it.

Of course, there were some more "interesting" people. Some guy said he was a movie producer and wanted to know if I would like to do some acting. I told him no; that I didn't have the time but thanked him. He pressed a little, saying it paid $40,000 a week. Thanks but no thanks. What a freak! I figured it was probably porn or something. I didn't have the Hollywood stars in my eyes that badly to get sucked into that. *Playboy* magazine is one thing—anything else is out of the question.

I stuffed everything I could think of for every contingency into my purse. I brought flip-flops in case the heel of my shoe broke, a change of outfits in case the one I was wearing got ruined, a shower cap in case I wanted to swim and not get my hair wet, my cell phone to call Bruce when to pick me up, lipstick, lip liner, and a black eyeliner pencil. I was prepared for the worst.

I did slip on my flip-flops to head out across the lawn to see his mini zoo. Can you imagine living in a house with your own zoo? And you know what an animal lover I am! Though it was dark and dimly lit there were lots of monkey and birds of every sort and color. As I pressed into the area further it looked like a fairy tale. It was the most beautiful place I had ever seen. A tropical rain forest in the middle of Los Angeles! The landscape was plush and green with that fresh, after-a-rain smell. Little droplets of water were clinging to the leaves, and there was a hush to the place as the waterfalls drowned out the sounds of the party, and beyond that the city noises of L.A. Waterfalls cascaded everywhere. It was so peaceful. I came to a pool with oversized double lounge chairs. I walked around to the front and found tons of gorgeous flowers planted in the center surrounding a fountain.

There were more areas of the mansion and grounds to see than I could wander in a week. I hadn't seen any part of the upstairs or the large guest area that was about as big as the mansion itself. I did get into the TV room where they played a movie once a week. I decided to leave and called Bruce. While going to find a quiet spot to make a call, there was a waiter playing with a cat that, when I tried to pet it, acted really strangely. Suddenly it thought the bottom of my outfit was a play toy and attacked the train. Eventually it released the fabric and went on its way. I headed out the door and, as soon as I started to move, the cat was back—even more tenaciously than the first time! I was sure the train of my outfit would have holes and pulls in it. It already had stains, from all kinds of drinks, from brushing on the ground. Even with my 6-inch heels, the gown still touched the ground. I did get lots of compliments on the dress from all of the girls.

Miss June left with John Lovitz in his BMW along with her three friends that I had hung out with a lot of the night . . . I took the shuttle home at 4:30 a.m., and Bruce, with a guy from the casino, picked me up and we went back to the casino. We flew home later that day at 1:00 p.m. That was a wrap.

P.S. I talked to Rhonda and asked her if she had noticed on Playboy.com that Drew Barrymore was there; that I didn't see her. She told me that I had stood right next to her. She was very tiny with reddish hair. Why didn't you tell me, I asked her? She didn't know I liked her so much. Next time I will pay closer attention!

The Playboy.com website even ran an article about the party I attended. They said the birthday bash is one of the toughest parties to get invited to, with a very limited number of invitees.

One thing that I did leave out of the above letter to my family was when I was in a back room above the workout gym, one girl asked if I partied. She told me I could join them. I looked down, and they were doing lines of white powder that I assumed was cocaine. However, considering that this was a Hollywood party, I frankly thought there might be more drugs or open sex. It was one thing I had been nervous about—I'm not a drug user.

Naturally my family would not have been thrilled to read this piece of information.

Chapter Five

My photo shoot was on March 5, 2002, and my pictorial for Playboy.com finally got published on April 11, 2002. The article was written, and it was published with my pictorial. The actual version of our collaboration can be found on the web. I could finally call myself a *Playboy* model. I was so proud! I told everyone! Everyone around me knew how hard I had worked, and they were excited for me. I even got a letter from my trainer:

I finally saw the pics! Great stuff! I'm so glad to see that dreams and goals and good thing happen to good people. I see a lot of kids every day, and they all have dreams and aspirations and 95 percent of them don't make it to the Big Leagues. It's tough to see, and a lot of kids get a lot out of their time and learn a great deal along the way, but everyone wants to meet their goals. You should be so proud of the achievement and your commitment. I know you made some sacrifices for this dream, and that makes it all the sweeter!
Yours in health,
Trent

My dad was not to be told because he would be very upset according to my mom. I was surprised but understood. I sent a thank-you letter and gifts to all that were part of my photo shoot. Naturally, I still wanted to appear in the *Playboy* magazine and I really did the .com shoot just so I would be able to be part of the *Playboy* family. It was a good thing to be able to put on my resume every time I contacted *Playboy*. It paid $750—but it cost me thousands to get there (not to mention all the surgery and working out!). I still was not done with Playboy. I noticed a section for *Playboy* Poker and decided to tell them my story to hopefully be used for their online poker section. I wrote to

care@Playboycasino.com *on May 8, 2002:*
I just did my exclusive pictorial for Playboy.com because I am a profes-

sional poker player and very well-known around the world and you can find me at www.Playboy.com/livinginstyle/guy101/poker. I am the Queen of Hearts for *Playboy*. Many of my gambling friends place bets on your site. When I told them that I had done a shoot for Playboy they all went to Playboysportsbook.com and figured I would be there. I would love to be so if you can use any of my pictures to help promote your site, please do.

It was time to put my next plan of action into play. I decided to call the *Playboy* mansion to ask if they thought that I would be invited to any more parties.

Jenny Lewis said, "If you were invited to the last one, you're probably sure to be invited to the next one."

"I'm willing to travel and pay for my own flight to go to the Mardi Gras *Playboy* party or the Vegas parties or anywhere really."

"Who am I speaking with?" Jenny Lewis asked.

"Jill Ann Spaulding."

"Jill Ann, Mr. Hefner was so disappointed that you didn't come up and introduce your self." I could hardly believe that she knew exactly who I was when I gave her my name.

"I did. I even got a picture with him," I told her. (I suddenly realized I did go up to him but I never told him my name; I just posed and was really intimidated and walked away as soon as the flash went off.)

"Oh. Well, he must have forgotten."

Suddenly I was filled with dismay. "I feel awful. I went up to him a couple of times, but I thought he might feel I was bugging him."

"Not in the least. He's not like that," she assured me.

"With so many guests I didn't think he would have known me."

Jenny laughed lightly. "Oh no, he was expecting you!"

I told her about my pictures having gone up on the website on April 11th. She wondered if they were from the party, but I explained they were done for an exclusive on Playboy.com. She indicated that Mr. Hefner would certainly want to see these. I gave her the web address, thanked her and hung up.

I wrote a letter to Mr. Hefner and included a picture of me on the way to the party as well as from the pictorial.

Dear Hef:

Thank you so much for having me to your birthday party. It was wonderful! April has been a completely amazing month for me with your party on April 6th and my pictorial on Playboy.com published on April 11th! Thank you

so much for everything. Hope to see you sooner than the next party.
   With love and luck
   Jill Ann Spaulding

What did I mean by that last sentence? I wanted to be one of the girlfriends who were sitting at the table. I had done some very dedicated research. I purchased the videos "Inside the Playboy Mansion." After being
turned away from the table at the party, I was determined to find out how to
become a girlfriend, who these girls are, and where they came from. There
was never one current girlfriend, ex-girlfriend, or long ago girlfriend who had
ever said anything bad about Hugh Hefner. I found that remarkable. Almost
all relationships end with negative feelings in some way or another. In Hugh
Hefner's case, ex-girlfriends still go to many of the parties and events. They
all are always kissing him, hugging him, and making a huge fuss over him. In
the video, the most the girls ever say about sex came from Buffy Tyler. She
said, "People ask about sex and I say I don't kiss and tell." The whole video
is very evasive on the subject.
   Here again, I wasn't naïve, but the "pajama party" atmosphere, and that
"Playboy sisterhood" again had me thinking that all those beautiful women
were for show. I assumed he had one special girlfriend, and the rest of the
girls were there to make him look sexy and desirable and powerful.
   Esquire Magazine *June 2002 by Wil S. Hylton quoted Hugh Hefner as
saying, "I have slept with thousands of women, and they all still like
me."*
   Time Out New York *by Adam Rapoport, in the issue on April 6-13,
2000, Hefner was quoted as saying, "The girls have become close friends.
It may be difficult to imagine, but there is no rivalry or jealousy . . . There
are Sandy, Mandy and Brande and Jessica, and they're the only girls I
see."*
   Brande Nicole Roderick became a Playmate of the month® April 2000
and Playmate of the year® 2001. Sandy and Mandy Bentley made the cover
and inside of the *Playboy* magazine in May 2000. I still was doing research
before I decided to pursue such a thing. On MarksFriggin.com they have
archives, and this is some of what it said: "On March 13, 2000, Brande
Roderick came to the Howard Stern show to talk to Howard. Howard asked
her many of details about having sex with Hef, and she didn't have many
answers. Brande said they all hang out and watch movies in bed with Hefner.
She said that she's never seen the other girls having sex with Hef but thinks
that they do. Most of the guys on the show didn't believe that she actually

does sleep with Hef. Howard believed her ,but asked her to swear that she does. She ended up saying, 'I swear on the Lord Jesus Christ that I sleep in Hugh Hefner's bed,' and then added that she has sex with him. KC and Gary still didn't believe her. Even Robin found it hard to believe what she was saying. After Brande swore to it, Robin said she wanted to get out of the studio before the lightning struck. KC told Howard, 'If she's sleeping with Hef then I'm Jesus.'"

MarksFriggin.com Archives read that Playmate Katie Lohmann was in the studio. Howard wanted to find out about her dating Hugh Hefner and if it was all true or not. Howard went on to ask Katie about the Hefner stuff. She was one of Hef's seven girlfriends, and Howard heard that's all hype. She said that she never had sex with him, but she's not sure about the other girls. She said she loved Hef but it was a "different kind of love" that she couldn't really explain.

Quoted from Designboom.com, May 5, 2001, Hefner was asked My Favorite Occupation. "I'm dating seven girls, and it is a wonderful, romantic relationship and at my age quite remarkable; Tina, Jennifer, Regina, Michelle, Elaine, Tiffany and Stephanie."

I decided it had to be an act. No rivalry, no jealousy—there had to be no sex. There was no way that all of these ex-girlfriends could be so happy, continue to go to the parties and never have anything bad to say about Hef. I believed it was a publicity idea for the magazine. It was every man's fantasy and to hold on to the *Playboy* image, he had to appear to be a true *Playboy*. I even discussed it with my grandpa, not in detail of course. I asked him whether he thought Hefner has sex with those girls. He was adamant that it was all for show. That was the extent of the conversation, but since I looked up to my grandpa it underscored what I believed.

I looked at the girlfriends that were on the video cover. Following is a brief biography of every girlfriend, dressed in lingerie, featured on Hef's bed:

Tina Jordan   Birthplace: North Hollywood, CA – 8/21/1972
5'5" – 115 lbs – 34DD-24-34. Playmate of the month® March 2002
Tiffany Holliday home is Los Angeles, CA – 9/15/1979
5'4" – 118 lbs – 34D-25-36. Cybergirl of the Week November 5, 2001
Buffy Tyler   Birthplace: Fredericksburg, TX – 4/18/1978
5'5" – 115 lbs – 36D-24-34. Playmate of the month® November 2000
Kimberly Stanfield   Birthplace: Vancouver, BC – 11/18/1981
5'6" – 106 lbs – 34C-24-34. Playmate of the month® July 2001
Katie Lohmann   Birthplace: Scottsdale, AZ – 1/29/1980
5'4" – 103 lbs – 32D-22-32. Playmate of the month® April 2001

I'm not certain who this last girl was, but all of these girls were listed as girlfriends, and all of them were Playmates except Tiffany Holliday, but she still lived at the mansion so maybe this had something to do with it. I had to become a girlfriend. I would have to commit to moving into the mansion to fulfill my dream. I figured that you had to put in your time for promoting and doing events before they made you a Playmate.

Here was a list of other girlfriends who were documented in articles and on Playboy.com and Playboy magazine as to be considered dating Hugh Hefner or considered one of his girlfriends. Stephanie Heinrich became the first cyber girl ever and Playmate of the month® in October 2001. Dalene Kurtis was Playmate of the month® September 2001 and then became Playmate of the year® 2002. Cathy O'Malley was a special editions model for Playboy. Christi Shake was Playmate of the month® May 2002. Charis Boyle was Playmate of the month® February 2003.

I know it sounds strange, because I was in a relationship, to consider being Hef's "girlfriend," but I considered it to be in name only. I was utterly convinced this was no different from TV stars and models needing to do promotional events. It was part of the package for promoting the *Playboy* name. I assumed the girls who became his girlfriends were part of an image of luxury, sexiness, and allure that made the rest of the world want to be part of the "Playboy mystique."

Chapter Six

On the tape *Inside the Playboy Mansion* Hef himself says, "There's room for one more." It seemed he was speaking to me. Believe it or not, my boyfriend and I actually studied the tapes together, discussed what I was going to do and, amazingly, he said that he didn't want to ever feel he held me back from my dream. He would be sad and miss me, but he would supervise the stores, the house and everything while I was gone. He knew I was the little girl who wanted all the glitz, glam, and excitement and he didn't want to stop me.

I decided to call Jenny at the mansion and try to get some information about how I could be a girlfriend without coming right out and asking.

"Hi, Jenny it's Jill Ann Spaulding calling. I sent Hef a letter and was wondering if he had said anything about it."

"What did you expect him to say?" she asked.

"Well, I mentioned that I would like seeing him sooner than the next party."

"He's a busy man. If you want to see him sooner than the next party, pick a time that you are going to be in the area and tell him about it," she offered.

I thanked her for the information and began to write. I didn't have a trip coming up, so I picked days that a good poker tournament was going on, and it would keep Bruce busy if I were asked to come up to the mansion. Bruce and I discussed my not coming back for a few months or more, and we agreed that if I were asked to move in that I could and I would. I didn't know if I would get a response or not.

Dear Hef,

I want to be with you. I know you do not have a lot of time to give, and I understand this up front. I am going to be in California June 5 to 10. I would love to stay at the mansion, if possible, during this time. Maybe I could watch old movies with you, your girlfriends, and others. You would have a chance to see the genuine warmth, compassion, and honest attraction I have for you,

Meeting Hugh Hefner for the first time.

Standing by the front door of the Playboy Mansion

First picture as I entered through the gates for my stay at the Playboy Mansion

My bedroom at the Playboy Mansion

Playboy Mansion fountain in front of front door.

Hugh Hefner "Fun in the Sun" Sunday during my stay. He is playing backgammon while all the girls are getting some sun.

Inside the Playboy Mansion where Hef is always seen giving interviews on this very same couch with his pictures of family, girlfriends and others in the background.

At Pussy Cat Dolls at the Roxy in Hollywood. Marilyn Manson and Hef.

and we might hit it off. I am willing to commit myself only to you and do nothing else for the time that you give me in your life.

With love,

Jill Ann

I used the exact phrase that Katie Lohmann said in the *Inside the Playboy Mansion* video. When she met Hef, she right away let him know that she wanted to be with him.

It was about June 1ˢᵗ and I had no response of any kind from anyone. I wasn't sure what to think when the phone rang. It was a security officer from the Playboy Mansion confirming my arrival from June 5 to 10.

I thought he was kidding. "Really?"

"Do you mean to tell me that no one has called you about this?"

"No, no one."

"Well, it's on my log that you will be staying in the guest house on those dates. Hef has asked you to accompany him and his girlfriends Wednesday the 5ᵗʰ and Friday the 7ᵗʰ."

"I really get to go?" I couldn't believe my ears. "What do I wear?"

He said, "Wednesday is club wear. Friday is too, but dressier."

I thanked him. He let me know that they really didn't take care of transportation to the mansion and that if I needed to be picked up he would need 24-hour advance notice. I let him know I would be driving my own vehicle, and he was glad to hear this. He told me to give my name to the guard at the gate when I got there, and someone would help me with my bags.

I don't think it sunk in right away, but it didn't take long. Now that it was really happening, I was very nervous and excited at the same time. A million things went through my head. I was spinning. What would I bring, what would I wear, how will I act? I started packing immediately trying to prepare. I selected nearly everything I owned. I set out half a dozen jackets, a dozen pairs of shoes—including my sexiest, many outfits, jewelry, my pillows, and even my makeup tape to be certain I had it just right. I packed enough clothes to stay a very long time. Bruce offered to send me clothes from the store so I could have new outfits when I was there if I was asked to stay on. He said he would take a plane home if I stayed since he had his own vehicle at our house. Bruce and I drove to L.A., and I dropped him off at Commerce Casino but not before going to the room and redoing my makeup so that it was fresh and perfect for my big entrance.

Now, just to let you know what a remarkable man Bruce is, I don't want to give the impression that he was thinking anything would happen sexually at the mansion. He supported my dream, but he knew *me—the real me. He knew that it was* several *dates before I even let him kiss me when we first got together, and it was six months before we slept together. He knew that my core values were rock solid, and we truly trusted each other.*

Bruce drew me a map and the exits I needed to get there. I had discussed with Bruce that I might get homesick right away and have to leave. He was supportive, as usual, and told me I would be fine.

Even with Bruce's directions, I still got a little lost and ended up at the back gate of the mansion. The gates are very high and wrought iron at the entrance. It's like driving up to a castle. I told the uniformed guard my name and, after making a call to verify, he said he would help me get to the front gate. The security guard jumped in his car, and I followed him to the front gate. He pushed the button to open the gate. In the rearview mirror, I could see him starting to walk up the path to the mansion. I backed up and asked if he wanted a lift up the drive. He smiled and got in. I couldn't resist taking a picture of me entering the famous gates. I had butterflies in my stomach, and my heart was hammering. This was both scary and thrilling. I was shown where to park my car, and a guy came out to help me with my bags. I noticed right away that this guy wouldn't give me much eye contact and didn't really seem to help me with my bags. I carried almost everything, and he seemed not to notice.

We walked to a small house, like a perfect little guest cottage, and went through a wooden door with a French Country feel. It opened to a nice little living room with a couch, TV, and computer. He showed me to my room. I tried to tip him, but he said he couldn't accept it. Shortly afterward he came back and gave me a key to the door. The room was great. I immediately felt comfortable. I looked out the windows. Two of them faced a tennis court, and the other two looked over the grounds, where I could see blooming flowers, lush foliage, and a rich green lawn the color of emeralds. I assumed they had a small army of groundskeepers to maintain the place to its impeccable condition.

I put away all the clothes in the closet and still had to go back out to my car for more things—I hadn't traveled light! When I walked through the door, a wall had a picture of Marilyn Monroe on it. I knew Hef was a huge fan of hers and had published very famous photos of her. The wall to the left had a very sexual picture of a man that looked like it could have been Hugh Hefner performing cunnilingus on a naked woman bent over backwards. I couldn't see the face well, but it had his look. The room also had a VCR, radio, and

CD player. There was a chest of drawers and a nice chest to put little items in. On both sides of the bed were small tables. One side held a telephone with a list of phone numbers for anything I needed from the mansion: room service, laundry service, maid service—everything. The other side was a pull-down desk and, when I lifted the cover, I found a printer underneath. No computer, though. It had a fairly roomy closet. There were many other pictures on the walls and two chairs. The most wonderful thing was the bed. It was so luscious with its down comforter and down pillows, so luxurious you sank down into them, and the whole ambiance of the bedroom was warm and wonderful.

I was very excited. I called Bruce right away and told him I had made it safely and described the room. He thought it sounded great. Then I called my mom and my grandma to tell them. For some reason, I felt at home right away. I think it was the feeling one gets when the dream starts moving toward reality. I sat in the bed and lay back feeling like a princess. The room was so clean and cute. I turned the TV on and tried to let it all sink in. I had put away everything in its place. I set up my makeup for easy access. I lined up all my shoes. I wandered into the bathroom. I could tell right away that I would be sharing it. Someone had all of her personal belongings set up and was definitely unpacked to stay. On the other side of the room from where I entered was a doorway that led to a room filled with pictures of a girl with many friends and a Zed card (a modeling card with a variety of poses on it) of a Michelle. I checked out the living room, looked at the computer, the artwork on the walls and then went out to the hallway to a separate room that was similar to an atrium. It had a sun roof and outdoor air coming in. There were many places to sit. I went through another door and could tell that there were two more guest rooms and the hallway led out to the back property of the mansion where the back security gate was visible.

I found my way back to my room and began to look at the list of people that I could call at the mansion. I found the line for room service. When I called I told them I was a new guest and I didn't know what kinds of things I could order or how to go about it. They told me that they didn't have a menu but that if I could think of it they could probably make it. I ordered a piece of chicken and a fruit plate. It would be ready in about half an hour but as they didn't have delivery service I would have to go to the kitchen myself and pick it up. They told me how to get there and I ventured out. I went in heels and my cutest-looking outfit just to pick up something to eat. I wasn't sure whom I would run into. I knew my way around a little bit from the birthday party, but nothing looked familiar. The night of the party had been a blur and jammed with people, so it's not surprising. I walked by the pool, and there was no one around. The entire grounds seemed to be deserted. I was surprised. I just assumed there would always be people in the pool and on the premises. Not today.

I followed the directions to the kitchen and only ran into workers and staff. They did not seem especially friendly, and none of them really acknowledged me. They showed me where to stand because my order wasn't quite ready and explained that they call the room as the order comes up so guests don't have to wait. I realized I hadn't ordered a drink. They showed me a glass-faced refrigerator with an array of drinks and let me choose whatever I wanted. I got a large tray and put my food on it. The fruit plate was as luscious with ripe fruit as at any five-start hotel, and I headed back to my room to eat. They had told me to leave the tray in the atrium as they don't come into guests' rooms. I was to call when finished, and someone would come out to retrieve it.

I watched TV a while and decided to call the security office to find out what time I was to go out with Hef and his girlfriends. I was told to be in the main room at the mansion at 10 to 10:15. I heard noises outside and when I peeked out I found a girl about twelve, a dog, and a boy in the living room. The girl said hello right away and asked why I was there. She wondered if I was a playmate or doing a test shoot. I told her I was staying here at Hef's invitation. She explained that her mom lived here and that she was Hef's girlfriend. The little boy left, and the girl explained that he was the son of one of the other girlfriends. I told her it was nice to meet her and went back to my room. I thought it was a little strange that children were there. I suppose I hadn't thought that some of the women—and girlfriends—might be moms.

Later on it became much louder in the other room, and I purposely stepped out to use the restroom as an excuse to see who the new arrivals were. Michelle, a very petite girl I guessed to be in her middle twenties, with whom I was sharing the bathroom, had come home. She asked me the same questions her daughter had. I picked up a funny feeling from her so I answered as positively as I could. In other words, I didn't tell the truth. She had a threatened look on her face when she asked me how I came to be there. I told her that I had written to Hef telling him about my pictorial for *Playboy* on Texas Holdem. I explained that I was a champion poker player and that I told him I wished I could have stayed at the mansion during the shoot like many of the girls have. I told her that I had asked him if I could stay for a few days since I didn't get to and it was approved.

I didn't say that I had come with the goal of staying and becoming a girlfriend. I didn't want her to feel threatened because I wanted to be accepted right away and have her let her guard down. Michelle told me she was an official Hugh Hefner girlfriend. I asked where all of the other girls were, and she told me they were inside the mansion. She chose to live out here because it was more private for her and her daughter to live. She stayed at the mansion Wednesday through Sunday and went back to her apartment Monday and Tuesday.

I told her, "That is so neat that Hef doesn't mind that you have a child; that this has no effect on him."

"Oh no," she said. "Jennifer is a girlfriend, and her son lives at the mansion as well."

I was surprised. "That is really cool. How many official girlfriends are there?"

"There are seven and many more that are not official."

"How do you know if you're official or not?" I wondered.

"Well, Hef takes you into his bedroom, opens up the safe and gives you a diamond *Playboy* necklace. He helps you put it on, and you know you're official."

I admired her necklace. It sparkled, and I have to say, it was something that you noticed right away dangling there around her neck, and she made sure to remind me that they were genuine diamonds. I wanted that necklace. I had one similar but this one was the authentic one and it was beautiful. I excused myself and went back to my room. I peeked out to ask what she suggested wearing for the evening. She told me I should select something I would wear to any club. We would be coming back here afterward. Nothing special happened on Wednesdays that I needed to know about. Fridays, however, there was a buffet dinner and an old movie and then we would go out on the town.

I ordered more food to make sure I was full for the evening's events. I followed protocol this time and, when I got back, Michelle invited me to eat with her and her daughter. I kept to myself and was careful of my manners. She went over the rules of the shared bathroom. The decorative towels were hers and not to be touched. The items in there were hers and not to be used. She showed me what was provided by *Playboy* and what her personal things were. I thanked her and finished eating while she and her daughter watched a show. I complimented her on her Zed card that was on her door and she told me that she had been on Baywatch and a soap opera.

"I can see where you must have been a success on TV. You're very beautiful."

"Thanks. My head is killing me tonight, though. I just had $1,200 worth of extensions put in and it sure hurts. I feel so gross. I can't wash them for a while and it's driving me crazy to feel dirty."

"Your hair looks great," I told her. The extensions gave her that "Playboy" look of lush hair that men just want to run their fingers through.

After I finished eating I retreated to my room and closed the door. I went back to shower and removed the days' makeup. I put hot rollers in my hair and closed the door. I watched my makeup video to make sure it was perfect for my big evening. I went all out with the makeup: fake eyelashes, contouring, highlights—the works. I put great smelling sparkle lotion all over and perfume. I was dressed to the hilt wearing my Betsy Johnson red and black dress with a very low-cut front. Betsy is a top designer known for playful, flirty, sexy clothes. The dress fit me to perfection. The necklace was diamonds around the neck and a chain that dropped past my chest. I wore my bunny earrings and a cute *Playboy* bracelet. I was ready to roll, and saying that I was nervous doesn't do it justice. I knew that I had to make a great impression and that I wanted him to really like me so that I could stay on and ultimately become a Playmate.

The time had come, and Michelle showed me where to go in the mansion. My heart was racing as more and more girls started to arrive. A few came down the grand staircase, and I thought of old movies like Sunset *Boulevard or* Gone with the Wind *with the type of staircase you can make an entrance on. I still had not seen or spoken with Hef. Finally, he came down the stairs. He didn't acknowledge me right away.*

I motioned to him. "Hi. I'm Jill Ann."

"I know who you are," he said with a big smile.

He walked away to get his drink—a Jack and Coke®, of course. He didn't say anything else to me, but suddenly all of the girls were motioned to get ready for pictures and, as if rehearsed, everyone rushed to their spots and I followed. Finding nowhere to stand I sat on my knees with three other girls below Hef and the pictures were taken by an in-house photographer. There was a total of thirteen girls. None of the girls acknowledged that I was even there except the obviously nonofficial girlfriends. They were extremely nice and friendly, but any girl who was wearing the official necklace did not make eye contact, including Michelle. So much for what I had read about no jealousy. Michelle had seemed so friendly out in the guest house, and suddenly I felt like she had turned on me. To say I felt a chill was an understatement, but I know that I am a sincere person, and I felt I could eventually win over these women.

One of the girls at least, named Kelly, was exceptionally nice and seemed to latch on to me right away. Since she was really the only one, naturally I talked back.

"Are you one of Hef's girlfriends?" I asked.

"Oh, no Hef and his girlfriends call me usually Tuesdays to invite me to go out with them on Wednesdays and call me Thursdays to go out on Fridays. I'm also called every week to come up for fun in the sun on Sundays."

"What's that?"

"It's where we all lay out by the pool and have dinner and a movie."

"That sounds really cool," I said. "Do they call you before every time you come up?"

"Yes." She pointed to a gal named Destiny, and said she also drove up when they call her.

She asked what my story was, and since she was not an official girlfriend I just told her that Hef asked me to stay for a few days and left it at that.

As soon as the pictures were taken, everyone immediately left the house and headed down the back way of the mansion. It was dark, and the concrete on the driveway was very uneven. I stepped on a rock and both Kelly and a gal named Destiny grabbed me before I fell. I was wearing very high heels that were killing me and very hard to walk in—the price we women pay for being sexy! All of us walked down the long path in the darkness to a huge SUV limo with a big *Playboy* bunny on the door. There would be no mistaking us as we drove down the road! There were many bodyguards to help us into the car and make sure we were in safely. All these men were very large and well-built, all dressed in "L.A. chic" with black shirts and dark pants. And all looked like you wouldn't want to mess with them. Again, as if rehearsed, all of the girls seemed to have a certain place that they sat inside the limo, and by the time I got in I was all the way up front with, of course, the five girls who didn't have official necklaces on. I didn't mind this and settled into the plush leather seats. I was going to make sure not to step on any toes or make the girls not want me part of their group.

Inside the limo, Hef started to take pictures of groups of girls. There was loud music playing party songs to get us all in the mood for clubbing, and flashing lights and straws for every drink so that the girls wouldn't mess their lipstick. Hef opened a bottle of Dom Perignon with a "pop" and started pouring it in glasses for all of us. I was quite impressed. I was like a little kid and opened up a bag of gummy bears and made myself at home. It was as though I had found my niche. I loved it. I never smiled so much. Since no one other than Kelly had showed any interest I decided to introduce myself hoping that if they felt I wasn't a threat they would open up to me. I assumed it was like high school. If I wanted to be part of a group of popular kids I had to have them feel I was on their level.

"I'm Jill Ann. I did an entire pictorial for *Playboy* in April because I'm a professional poker player. It's nice to meet everyone, and I want to thank all of you for having me with you."

The music was loud, but I tried to speak over it. The response I got was complete silence. At the moment, I felt completely stupid, but I still hoped they would accept me. When we arrived at the club, Hef stepped out of the limo and helped each girl exit the car, following all of us into the club. Bodyguards were at the front and back of the line. They cleared the way for our big entrance and helped to make certain we entered safely. People were taking pictures, and I felt like a celebrity. Behind the velvet rope—on the other side—were people in their best outfits trying to get admitted to the club, but of course with Hef we were just instantly squired in. Everyone was looking at me. All the security, the limo, the pictures—it was a dream come true. I reflected on my guest room, the maid service, room service, laundry service, a great place to stay, the mansion, a place where celebrities hang out—I was sold! This was a lifestyle I could get used to!

We arrived at our roped-off table to find gigantic bottles of Evian and champagne glasses. As soon as we were seated, one of the bodyguards was instructed to take a picture of us. Again, every girl seemed to have a predetermined spot next to Hef, and the five unofficial girls tried to get in the picture. It was strange, like learning a new language or something . . . everyone else seemed to know what to do, and I was trying to learn as I went along. A waitress took our order—we could drink anything we wanted. I didn't want to overindulge and preferred to stay sharp. All of us didn't say much. The music was loud, and I was very excited.

I looked around our table. These were women with a certain look—like the one I had achieved. They were in sexy clothes that showed off toned legs and tan bodies. Each had her hair freshly styled. If her hair was long and straight, it had obviously been done with a flat iron to get the "movie star" silky look (or they were extensions). If they opted for a curlier look, they were those fluffy gorgeous curls most women would kill for. Not one face was marred by imperfection, and the makeup all wore was perfectly done to show off high cheekbones and exotic eyes. Some were platinum blondes—that white blonde that turns heads. Though the process to get platinum hair can be brutal on the hair itself, these women obviously took advantage of expensive hair treatments to keep it silky and soft.

I bent to Kelly's ear. "Wow. Look at all the guys staring over here." No wonder, I thought to myself.

"Oh, God, don't look," she said.

"Why not?" I was puzzled.

"Hef gets very upset if you aren't giving full attention to him. Even if you see someone you recognize, don't acknowledge them."

I believed her. She didn't look around at all and when I actually paid attention, none of the official girlfriends were looking around. I made sure that for the entire night I didn't look anywhere but at Hef and the girlfriends. Again, it was like trying to learn something totally new. I promised myself I would be more observant.

Kelly said, "If you need to go to the bathroom, there is a special one for us and you have to be escorted by a bodyguard."

I needed to go, so she went with me to show me what to do. On the way, I tried to make a little small talk with the bodyguard without much response. When I got inside the bathroom I mentioned to Kelly about the bodyguards seeming cold. She told me that they aren't supposed to interact with us; we are Hugh Hefner's dates, not theirs. I said it seems the same way at the mansion with the butlers and staff. She said they are not supposed to have eye contact with you or talk to you about anything but the most necessary things. I got the message. Once finished we were escorted back to the table by the bodyguard.

Hef hadn't said one word to me since the greeting at the mansion. We were all getting drinks. Hef stood up and said, "Let's dance."

Everyone got up and moved to the floor. The girls ordered shots and drank them readily. I managed to avoid drinking at all. I wanted to be in full control and hid the fact I wasn't partying like the rest of them. As a poker player, I knew to keep my wits about me at the table—smart gamblers don't drink at the table. Now I was gambling to be a Playmate, and I wanted to stay sharp. Hef was dancing around with different groups of girls, and then he came over to me and gave me a great big smile. I had watched all the party tapes of the mansion galas and noticed that every single girl kissed him on the mouth. I had planned this and was ready.

I kissed him on the lips and said, "Thank you so much for having me here."

He didn't respond but smiled again. The smile seemed genuine, and he looked like he was having a good time. He got into the rhythm of the music that was pulsing. Other girls came near, and we all started dancing and then I felt him put his hand on my butt. I suddenly felt out of my element—like someone working undercover. I was doing something for a goal and had to act the part. No one had touched me except Bruce for many years, but I couldn't give that away. I was not unhappy that he touched me. He was the most powerful man in the world of my dreams that I had held on to for so many years. All the girlfriends would kiss him and dance sexily with him. It was all an act for his image. I figured the seventy-six-year-old guy probably couldn't get it up anymore and that he hadn't for a long time and that was why no girlfriends were mad at him. Later in the evening he came over to me again and was dancing with me. He kissed me on the mouth, and I asked Kelly to take a picture of us dancing together. Without him saying one word, he motioned to Kelly that it was okay to take the picture and at that moment he put his arms around me, clinching my right breast, and we were cheek to cheek for the picture. I asked Kelly to also take one with my camera.

"After this, I and my girlfriends go upstairs and party. We would like you to join."

I said just one word. "Sure."

I was having a blast, but it was still hard not to look around to see who was watching us. About a half hour after this brief conversation, it was suddenly time to leave. All of us were escorted in a line by bodyguards to the limo, Hef at the rear. I assumed my position up in the front of the limo.

Kelly whispered to me, "Hef would like you to come upstairs with him and his girlfriends when we get back to the mansion."

"He said that to me when we were dancing, but I didn't know what would happen for sure."

"He really likes you. You're so beautiful and nice. I wish you were one of them."

"Well, if I become an official girlfriend I'll ask them to invite you every time we go out."

She was incredulous. "Really?"

"Yes. You're so nice and fun. You're terrific." Kelly was so enthused she was smiling from ear to ear.

She said, "When you get back to the mansion you won't have to do anything. You can just watch. You don't have to participate. I'll guide you through the entire time, and I'll be with you all the way. Hef told me personally to take care of you."

I was unbelievably excited to find out what happened "upstairs"—this mythical place of legend. I had no idea what to expect.

I was excited and very curious. We all left the club and I was ushered into Hef's luxurious limousine—designed to get us noticed. I noticed Hef passing out a pill of some kind to his girlfriends in the limo. In a whisper, I asked Kelly what he was giving them, and she said I had to be an official girlfriend before I would get one. The limo headed back to the mansion. Expensive champagne—flowed, and girls, one dressed sexier than the next and all voluptuous, were hanging all over Hef. The music intense and I could feel the base shaking my whole body. The flashing lights inside the limo made me feel like I was on a disco floor. We pulled up to the outside gates of the back of mansion, got out, and proceeded to walk up the long mansion drive in the dark, and headed in through the mansion's front door and all walked up the stairs. The girls went in different directions—not straight into Hef's bedroom. Kelly took me quickly through a very large walk-in closet filled with Hef's pajamas, memorabilia, pictures and tons of clothing. We walked through quickly, but I tried to look around. The whole mansion was like no place I had ever been before, and I was awed by all of the items in the closet. Kelly went to a section in the closet where many nicely cleaned pink pajamas hung as she handed me a set on a hanger.

Then she led me to a gigantic marble bathtub.

"First, you have to take a bath."

I felt scared. Kelly saw it in my eyes.

"Don't worry," she said. "You only have to participate if you want to. It's hilarious and you won't ever forget it. When you're older you can write a book!"

She took off her clothes and started to run the water in the tub. I slowly removed my jewelry and shoes.

While the warm water ran, she started to whisper quietly to me as she helped me undo my dress.

"We're going to go in and sit on the bed. If you don't want to participate just keep your bottoms on. Otherwise, take them off. I'll be with you the entire time, and we'll stay together. I'm going to pretend to give you oral sex and you can touch me, or kiss me or whatever you're comfortable doing. All the girls will be around us doing the same thing. They're all faking it. No one is bisexual so don't touch another girl unless she touches you. If you watch you'll be able to tell that they're totally acting—nothing is really going on. Just follow my lead and you'll be fine."

I started to relax. In my mind, I talked to myself. I knew it. *I knew it. I can do this. I can pretend to kiss another girl. No problem. I can handle this. He probably just sits there and watches all of us,* I thought to myself. I assumed it was all for show, like a put-on private striptease. On some level, I naively thought it was about showing off our bodies, but not actually *doing* anything sexual.

A girl named Amber came into the bathroom and asked us what we wanted to drink. I ordered a diet coke and Malibu. Kelly had the same. Kelly was now in the bathtub, washing herself with sexy-smelling soap. She got out of the tub, and a girl named Britney got in. This was a cleansing ritual done by every girl invited upstairs. All the official girlfriends were supposed to be doing the same thing in their own personal bathrooms.

Deborah came into the bathroom and did not look thrilled to see me. I didn't want to get my hair wet and Kelly diffused the situation by asking if Deborah had a hair clip. Deborah gave me one, and I thanked her over and over again. Deborah was near the sink with a stack of hand towels, and she was soaking them in water and wringing them out before placing them in a bowl.

"What am I supposed to do?" I asked as I got into the tub.

"Wash under your arms, privates, and elsewhere, just like a regular bath."

"This isn't regular for me."

Suddenly Hef came into the bathroom with a camera. I felt a little shocked, and Kelly asked if it was okay if he took a picture. I said "Sure." He took a picture of Britney and me naked in the tub.

All of the girls seem to have vanished, and it was just Kelly and me in the bathroom together. The room echoed as we spoke with the marble all around us. I went to the restroom and took my time. I was very nervous. Amber came rushing in and told us to hurry up; everyone was waiting for us. Kelly grabbed my hand and led me into the main bedroom of Hugh Hefner. It was very dark. The only light came from two gigantic big screen TVs. Extremely loud techno music was playing. On the big screen TV's was anal guy porn very graphic and lots of noise of the people on camera having sex.

I was fully dressed in my pink pajamas, and there was a gigantic group of girls circled around Hef's bed with buzzing vibrators in each of their hands. Hef was in the middle.

Amber said, "Take off your clothes."

I was a little startled, but I took off my shirt and threw it behind me on the floor. Kelly took a spot on the side of the bed and motioned for me to join her. The drinks arrived, and Amber was holding a tray. Kelly asked her to hand us our drinks.

She did, with a sarcastic, "Will there be anything else?"

I didn't think much about it. I was too busy looking up at the mirrored ceiling and Hef naked in the middle of the bed, fully erect, making out with his main girlfriend, Deborah. He definitely looked old—He was almost neon white with no tan at all. With clothes on he seemed to look okay, but with his clothes off he looked not appealing.

The girlfriends were all using vibrators on their private parts. My heart was about to leap out of my chest. Everyone was topless except Amber. My heart was hammering and felt like it would burst out of my chest.

Kelly helped me get my own vibrator. One of the girls complained that mine was tangled in hers, and Kelly moved me to release her cord. I was one girl away from Hef with my body against the headboard. I was not a foreigner to a vibrator and put it to me. Each girl was panting or moaning, making noise like porn stars. I concentrated on remembering the room, palatial and imposing.

Once all of us were settled Kelly whispered to me. "As soon as Deborah starts giving him a blow job, I'm going to pretend to go down on you."

I was wide-eyed and assessed the situation. He must have sex with his main girlfriend and everyone else pretends to be having sex until they're done. I can handle this. I can do this. I'm okay. I was convinced that I could definitely do this to be a girlfriend and a Playmate. Hef lit up a rolled cigarette and passed it around. I waved it by, wanting to stay in complete control of the situation. Once the rolled cigarette had been passed to everyone, Deborah started giving Hef a blow job. She moved expertly up and down his penis, with Hef moving her hair back so he could see her motions better in the mirrors.

All of the girls partnered up and started making a lot of noise and pretending they were having girl-on-girl sex. Kelly put her head in my lap. She never did anything to me but made noises like she was. Out of the blue, Amber yelled at Kelly and said it looked like she was faking it. I was terrified and felt like I had been caught in school doing something wrong. Amber was trying to get us into trouble with Hef. Again, so much for the myth that there was no jealousy or rivalry!

I was busy staring up at the ceiling. Hef was watching me, and it looked like he liked that I was watching.

Kelly would not be quiet. She kept saying things like "they aren't really kissing" or "she isn't really doing such and such to her." After Deborah finished with the blow job she got on top of Hef and slowly descended on his penis. She moaned as she slid down him and then rode him for about two minutes. When she was done she took one of the warm plush towels and wiped his penis off. She applied baby oil on his penis and then she strapped on a large fake penis and started stroking it, standing up holding onto the bed frame and making a lot of noise. She didn't partner up but acted in control of herself, like a woman who knows how to put on a show for her man. Some of the girls were spanking each other, and you could hear the sound of hand striking flesh. Then one of the other girls moved across the bed to Hef and got on top of him.

I couldn't stop my heart. What had I gotten myself into? What did I do now?

I turned to Kelly. "They don't use any protection!"

"No."

I was shocked. I couldn't believe it. This girl slid slowly up and down Hef, occasionally leaning down and letting her platinum hair sweep sexily across his chest. Michelle, my roommate, went next and had sex with him without protection for about two minutes. All the girls in the room were yelling. "Fuck her, dad. Fuck her hard. Oh, what a big cock. Oh, ride her, daddy. Give it to her, daddy." This went on through every single girl that rode him. Some were very seductive, some played it up to the mirrors. Some moved faster, and still others were arching back, letting him get full view of their bodies.

All of the girls had sex with him while he was lying on his back except one girl they called China Doll. She was an Asian girl with extremely long, black hair that shone glossy thick. He got up on top of this girl and had sex with her in that position, gazing into her eyes. Deborah wiped off Hef's penis between each intercourse. When Hef got up on China Doll, Kelly said quietly to me that this would really piss off the other girls. He didn't get on top of anyone else. Kelly was keeping a continuous monologue to distract me or keep me focused that this was really hurting Deborah. She was the only one who really loved Hef, and it killed her to watch him have sex with all of these girls. It was true that the room seemed to go quiet when he had sex with China Doll. The usual cheering was not happening. It seemed that all the girls were letting Hef know of their disapproval.

Kelly said to me, "I have to go and thank Hef for the BMW he bought me. I'll be right back. You'll be okay."

She went over and gave Hef a blow job but didn't have intercourse with him. She came back, and we continued to play girl-on-girl acts.

She asked, "Do you mind if I kiss your breasts?"

"No," I said. She began to lick my nipples and suck on me motioning me to touch her and to do the same to her. I did. This was the first time I had ever done this. She kissed me on the lips but without any tongue. I was thinking that this was okay. I had experienced a lot this evening; first orgy, first seeing someone having sex in front of me, first having to pretend to have sex with a girl, kissing a girl, what was next?

Kelly said, "You want to have sex with him. It is a major honor. The girls are tested often."

"I think I'll play hard to get."

"He doesn't play that way. He's old and doesn't need the challenge. He has girls willing to sleep with him anytime."

"I'm okay right now. Aren't you afraid he'll hear us talking? "

"No. He can't hear with this loud music playing."

I was so worried about being in trouble or someone hearing what we were talking about. I wasn't going to be participating so I figured might as well watch because no one would believe me once I left the mansion that all this was going on. Amber didn't have sex with him and neither did Amanda. Kelly just gave him a blowjob. Seven girls all rode him for their two minutes. Deborah took a new towel out of the bowl after each girl had sex with Hef and she then proceeded to wipe off Hef's penis putting the used towel in a different bowl. She then applied new baby oil to his penis for each new girl. I guess the towel was their form of protection. I knew they didn't test me. I could have had sex with him. Who knew what, if anything, I had? This was crazy!

After all of the girls were done with him Deborah took a large bottle of baby oil that had a label "Hef's Baby Oil" on it and poured a huge amount down her back. It slid down seductively and her back glistened. Then she had anal sex with Hef. All the girls were in the background screaming, "Fuck her up the ass. Put your big cock up her ass. Give it to her." I was shocked, not so much by the act itself—though that surprised me—but because I also knew anal sex carried with it the highest risk for AIDS and other diseases. He slowly slid his penis into her, and she clearly was used to this as she didn't grimace or react in pain.

Hef finally spoke. "My cock is up her ass." He started making strange noises. After about two minutes, he withdrew, and his penis was still fully erect. He began to stroke himself and made all kinds of graphic noises, almost rehearsed, like in porno movies. Yet he seemed lost in his own fantasy. He was jacking himself off, and when he climaxed his legs jumped all around and he kept holding on to himself and making a lot of noise.

As soon as he had ejaculated, he lay back down, and he and Deborah started making out on the bed as if no one else was in the room, and at that point all the girls removed themselves and disappeared. I found my way back to the bathroom and started putting back all of my clothes and jewelry on. Kelly was still with me and she showed me where to throw the pink pajamas. Deborah came into the bathroom with all of the vibrators in hand and was washing all of them.

I asked her if she needed help, and she waved me off. I finished getting dressed and headed down the stairs with Kelly.

I said, "He gave you a BMW?"

"Oh, God," she said. "Don't tell anyone. None of the other girls know, and they would be pretty mad."

"I'm not going to say anything." I reassured her.

She told me that she had driven in and hinted about coming to my room, but I didn't know if I was allowed visitors. She understood. We swapped phone numbers and said goodnight. I headed back to the guest house. Michelle's daughter was in the living room watching TV, and I could tell Michelle was in the shower. I went to my room and closed the door. I immediately called Bruce from my cell phone and told him everything. I spoke as quietly as I could in case someone was listening. I didn't go into great detail but told him the highlights.

"Oh my God, you're not going to believe this. He has sex with all of those young girls!"

"You're kidding. How do you know? Did they tell you that?"

"Bruce, I saw it with my own eyes. Hef invited me to go upstairs with him and his girlfriends. They made me put on these pajamas and take a bath. Then they led me into the main bedroom, and there was porn on the TV and girls all around Hef's bed and each of them had a vibrator. He was in the middle with an erection and his main girlfriend started blowing him and then all of the girls were pretending to have sex with each other and making all kinds of noise, screaming things. Then each girl had sex with him and then, at the very end, he had anal sex with Deborah. After that, everyone left."

"Did he touch you?" Bruce wanted to know.

I told him, "No, not at all. I kept my underpants on and that was a signal that I was not participating. Hef took a picture of me and other girls naked in the bathtub. The girls said he would give me a copy of it. Hope I get one. Oh, yeah! He lit a rolled cigarette and passed it around."

"Did you smoke it?"

"No. He gave the girlfriends pills when we were riding in the limo."

I was talking a mile a minute and Bruce didn't say much—he let me get it all out. When I told him the story it wasn't in any particular order. Sometimes I remembered details that I just plugged in when I could catch my breath.

Suddenly there was a knock on the door. I told Bruce I would call him later. When I opened the door I found Michelle standing there. She invited me to join them in the living room. They had a little dog—that made me happy. The biggest thing I was missing was my puppy. The dog jumped in my lap and petting him made me feel more comfortable and relaxed.

She sent her daughter to bed and turned to me. "Oh, I feel so gross."

"Don't worry. You get to have your hair washed tomorrow."

"No. That's not what I mean. I haven't had sex with Hef in a while but I knew if I didn't he would be mad." She seemed embarrassed that I had seen her having sex with him. I pretended I didn't hear her.

"I saw him handing out those pills. What do they do?"

"They're supposed to relax you. If you watch you'll see I pretend to take it and slip it into my purse."

We ended sitting up for quite a while. I said, "Wow. That was pretty wild!" I referred to the evening upstairs.

She said, "The first time I went up there I started crying and was completely traumatized. If I had had any idea of what went on up there I would never have gone."

"How did you get involved in this whole thing, anyway?"

"My best friend, Tina Jordan, brought me into the group. She had been dating Hef for a long time."

"Didn't she tell you what happens up there?"

"No, and she knew I would never have gone up there if I had known."

I nodded. She said, "I'm thinking about moving out. I just can't put up with everything anymore. You know, my car broke down and Hef gave me the money to fix it, but he doesn't give me a weekly allowance anymore like he does all the other girls. He doesn't think I need the money, I guess, because of the royalties from Baywatch and the soaps. It's not really fair that one of the girls has a newer car than I do. I have an older Mercedes, but I've been here a long time. I deserve more. It's not good to have my daughter here, and I just don't really feel that Hef cares about me."

"Oh, I think he does. Did you have to pay for your hair extensions?"

"Oh no, there is an open account at two salons that we can use for anything we want except a makeup artist. We used to have that service anytime we wanted, but they are cutting back. I get all the services for free. I can even eat there."

I was impressed. "That saves a lot of money. Nice. That would be pretty expensive. Do you get a clothing allowance?"

"Yeah, because we go out so many times I needed a lot of different outfits. I go to cheaper stores so that I have a little extra that doesn't go to clothing."

"That's smart," I said. "You should just go to him and tell him you need more money. Show him what you get from the residuals of the shows so he knows. . . Which are the girlfriends?"

She listed them. "Jennifer, Deborah, Amber, Amanda, Nicole and Sarah who you haven't met because she just had a nose job and she's still in bed upstairs recovering."

"So there are seven." She nodded. "What about Destiny, Britney, and Kelly?"

"Britney is here shooting to be a playmate, and Destiny and Kelly are only invited up to have sex with Hef. Both those girls are disgusting and nasty. You notice that I had sex with Hef right away. I do that to go before those two. I don't trust them. Who knows what they might have?"

"Well, that's smart. So, they won't be girlfriends?"

"God, no. Hef has us seven, and he told us that he won't be changing or adding any girlfriends."

"Oh." You can imagine what I was feeling with that news. On the other hand, after what I witnessed, I no longer knew what to think. I was confused and still shocked.

"Many girls come up and sleep with Hef and that's that. They don't become girlfriends. Just like tonight. You could have had sex with him, and it wouldn't have mattered. Many girls give it up to him and are broken-hearted. They don't know what they might have caught, and they're still not made a girlfriend—only invited up on sex nights, or never again at all."

"Thanks for telling me. I won't be participating because they don't use protection. Too bad . . . it seemed like a terrific, exciting lifestyle and really a lot of fun. I've only slept with less than a handful of guys. In this day and age, I can't take the chance."

"I'd only slept with five guys by the time I had sex with Hef."

"Really."

"Yeah, but I've had problems since . . . always having UTIs."

When I didn't know what that was she explained she got urinary tract infections. "My urine had blood in it. I was on heavy antibiotics."

I had never had this and really didn't know what it was. I wondered if some of the other girls might have something. She said, "I hope not."

"You know, if I move out I won't have enough money to support my girl. It would be very hard."

I didn't know what to say. "I think Hef really does love you."

"You think so?"

"Yeah, don't you see the way he looks at you when he dances with you?" Of course, I was making this up to console her.

"I hate having sex with him. I dread it. But I'm a single mom. I'm stuck."

"Hey, don't dread having sex with him. You've already exposed yourself. Go up there with a positive attitude. Look at it as though it's a sisterhood and that you're having the time of your life!"

I didn't know what else to say to her. She didn't know anything about me and if I said anything negative about my upstairs experience I was sure it would have gotten back to Hef and then I would really be in trouble. More than I felt I already was. I realized that we had talked for a long time. Not once did she ask me anything about myself. She just needed someone to talk to, so I listened and gave her positive responses. She didn't know where I lived, what my past was, if I had kids—nothing. She wanted something from me—approval maybe, or someone to tell her what she was doing didn't make her a bad person or a bad mother—and I was willing to act it out.

"My ex-husband knows that I'm dating Hef but doesn't know the extent of it. If he ever found a nude picture of me he would sue for full custody. "That's why you'll never see me nude at any party, in a picture or otherwise."

"I don't know if I'm really thinking about getting out," she said. "There are so many rules and games. I'm just sick of it. Oh, if you want to call anyone don't call from the mansion phone. They're all bugged, and my room has a camera in it."

I couldn't believe it. "Is there a camera in my room, too?"

"I don't know, but I know where mine is. If you use the computer in this room, they can read what you write, so don't write anything you wouldn't want them to read."

This was crazy. All I could think about was all of the things I had already said to Bruce about what had happened upstairs and how I had called him all day. Everything that I had done in the room went through my head. I tried not to act flipped out about it, but I was absolutely freaked!

I tried to change the subject. "I noticed that all of the girlfriends have a little dog similar to yours. Did Hef give it to you?"

"No, I happened to have him before I got involved with Hef."

"See, you were meant to be a girlfriend. You had the same breed. Listen, Michelle, I really need to get some sleep."

I had begun to feel a personal connection to her. I felt involved. I admit I hadn't opened to her at all, just listened. I did feel for her, and I couldn't imagine how scared you would be to make certain that both you and your child were supported. I knew no matter what happened I had a rock solid supportive relationship. I showered and removed my makeup and headed to the bedroom. Of course I called Bruce and told him that my room might be bugged and I would tell him more when I saw him.

Bruce exploded. "What the hell is going on over there?"

"Don't worry. I'm fine. I'll be fine."

The next morning I washed my face and ordered breakfast. I used my makeup video and by the time I was done breakfast was ready. I ate in the designated area adjacent to the kitchen. I was alone. There didn't seem to be anyone up except me. No one walked by, and no one came down the stairs. I walked outside by the pool. There was a Miller Lite party going on. I stopped and wandered through the crowd and noticed there were lots of Playmates giving tours around the mansion. Naturally, being camera happy, I decided to get pictures of all the Playmates individually for my memory collection. I was very excited to meet them, and it was also a chance to look around the mansion. I followed the girls giving tours and got to see lots of the grounds, the game room, the zoo, the grotto, tennis courts. That was more in line with what I thought the mansion would be like; lots of guys and playmates wandering the estate. Everyone was very tastefully dressed, which surprised me. At the head of the pool, I recognized Hefner's physician, from the "Inside the Playboy Mansion" video. He was heading towards me.

Being Hef's doctor I figured that he was going to tell me that he needed to test me, or something. He introduced himself.

Out of the blue I said, "You don't have to worry about me. I've been with the same guy for ten years and I don't have anything."

He looked at me. "What in the hell are you talking about?"

"Oh. I went out with Hef last night and I thought you had come over to tell me you needed to test me or something."

He became absolutely enraged. "I don't know who you are. I don't care who you are. I don't care what you do or don't do with Hef."

"I'm so sorry. One of the girls said that everyone was tested often. I thought you were coming over here for that."

He said, "They aren't tested."

I looked at him with amazement. I'm sure I had that deer-in-the-headlights look. "Let's start over, please. I'm Jill Ann. I'm a professional poker player and I did a pictorial for *Playboy* on Texas Holdem."

"Texas Holdem? You know," he said, "I often have a no-limit Texas Holdem game at my house with a $5,000 buy-in. If you're interested I'd be happy to have you come."

I wouldn't enter a game with this much of a buy-in, but I didn't tell him that. I acted very interested. With the common ground of mutual interest, we chatted a while on the subject. He had calmed down from our initial encounter and was much nicer to me. I apologized again.

He said, "I do care, and I am interested." He said something to the effect that if I decided to indulge in sex with Hef he wished me good luck and shook his head as he walked away.

I was already hungry again since I was keeping to my healthy regimen. I picked up my order and went back to the guesthouse. I called Kelly, told her of my encounter and asked her if she had been tested. She hadn't, and I wondered who had told her the other girls had been. She said she had just assumed. I didn't understand. If she hadn't been tested why would she assume everyone had been? I needed to hang up. I wasn't sure if my room had ears, and I didn't want anyone to hear what I was talking about.

Michelle and her daughter were out and about in the living room. I ate in there with them to see if I could get any more information.

"What're you doing today?" I asked her.

"Nothing but tonight, Hef, the girls and I are going to the Pussy Cat Dolls and then dinner."

"I wonder if I'm invited."

"You should ask Hef."

"How do I do that?"

"Well, he's up working in the office doing his scrapbook. You could probably talk to him there."

"Will you show me where his office is?"

She agreed and made a phone call to someone. She needed to go to the salon to have her hair deep conditioned and wanted company. I told her I would go with her if she wanted. So she called the salon and made an appointment for me as well. I was excited to be going to a salon with an official girlfriend. That was what it was all about for me.

"Will you show me where Hef is?"

We walked out of the guesthouse and up some back stairs in to the mansion. She pointed down a hallway and told me he was at the end of it. The hallway walls were covered with pictures of old Playmates and events that had happened at the mansion. Walking down was like looking at a history of the sexual revolution. I finally got up enough nerve to head down the carpet. I passed by many doors, all of which were closed but the last one, at the end.

I walked in and said softly to the woman at the desk, "Hi. I'm Jill Ann Spaulding. I'm staying at the guesthouse, and Michelle told me that the group was going out to dinner tonight. I was wondering if I was invited."

"Hef hasn't informed me."

"Okay. I just wanted to check."

She said, "You're invited tomorrow night for buffet dinner, movie, and then going out afterwards."

I was thrilled. "Oh, thank you! Is there something I should be doing today?"

"No. There's a party going on held by Miller Lite. I doubt they would mind if you joined them."

As I headed out of the office I noticed one of the doors that I had passed on the way was now open. I could see Hef sitting in a meeting with two people looking at large pictures that might have been proofs for the magazine. My heart was pounding as I walked past back to where Michelle was standing. I stood in front of Michelle for a moment. She looked at me, puzzled.

"Heck with it," I said and walked back to Hef's office.

"Hef, can I go out with you and the girls to dinner tonight?"

He looked at me and smiled. "Yes, darling."

I practically skipped down the hallway and headed down the stairs to return to the guesthouse. Michelle was already at the bottom.

"How did it go?" she asked.

"He said yes!"

The expression on her face was surprised, threatened and incredulous— all at the same time. All she said was, "Oh."

Apparently this was not cool. I told her exactly what I had said. I could feel her hackles rise. She wasn't fooling me. I asked her what time dinner was, and she told me that they were leaving at 6:00.

We went up to the front of the mansion, and the valet brought up her Mercedes. As we headed for the mall she said there was a great store with terrific clothes with good prices. She needed to run there for some new out-fits. We spent about an hour and a half shopping. At one point, I couldn't find Michelle for about half an hour. She was nowhere in the store; I looked in the dressing rooms, back room, everywhere. I thought she had left me there. I felt sick. Finally, I spotted her.

"I thought you ditched me. I was trying to figure out how to get back to the mansion. I don't have the address with me."

"I wouldn't have done that to you," she assured me.

I called both my mother and grandmother to tell them what I was doing and let them know I was fine. I didn't call Bruce. I hadn't told Michelle that I had a boyfriend. I figured she was gathering information on me as it was, and I wasn't going to give anything more if I didn't need to.

I hung up from talking with my mom. Michelle said, "Wow. . . . It must be nice to be able to tell your family the truth. My family wouldn't understand. Just the mention of the Playboy mansion would set them off."

"Both my mom and grandma have always loved *Playboy*, and they're very supportive."

The salon was called Prive at 7373 Beverly Boulevard in Los Angeles. The valet took the car. There was an outdoor restaurant as part of the salon, and I ordered an iced tea and something small to eat. After lunch, I had my hair conditioned and decided that since this was a big occasion I would have my makeup done. The salon was obviously a place frequented by actresses. It was sexy and modern inside, and all the stylists seemed to really know what they were doing. I told the makeup artist it was important and that he needed to make enough time for me. He assured me over and over again it would be perfect that he would have plenty of time. He had me remove my makeup before having my hair done. He said that waiting until my hair was done would spoil it. (I didn't know it at the time, but I was being set up.) The same person doing Michelle's hair was doing mine as well so they had me stay longer under the heat because her hair wasn't finished. It took an extremely long time to blow dry my hair, and I started to get very nervous about running out of time. It was five o'clock when my hair was done. The makeup artist said he couldn't fit me in.

Michelle said, "I have to go back and change. I can't wait for you. You look fine without makeup anyway."

I started crying and on the way back to the mansion I decided not to go. I didn't want Mr. Hefner to see me without makeup. I absolutely was not going out on the town.

"Hef doesn't like girls who wear makeup. You look fine," Michelle said.

I did not look fine. As we traveled, I started to think about what I would have to do to still be able to go. When we pulled up I didn't even take my purchases from the car. I dashed to my room, threw off my clothes, washed my face and started to change into the outfit I had decided upon. I noticed a yellow note attached to my TV. "6/6 Jill Ann: The departure time for this evening has been changed to 8:30. Norma Maister." I started screaming. I was so excited and relieved. I came out and told Michelle. She didn't seem too pleased. So much for her little trick.

She said, "It's ridiculous that they didn't inform me. I'm pissed."

I returned to my room and started applying my makeup. At 8:30, everyone had gathered in the entrance to the mansion, pictures were taken, and we headed down the dark path to the limo. There weren't as many girls as usual, but again each girl was dressed sexily, in a way that drew attention. Each woman could have been in a shampoo commercial—everyone's hair was either sleek and shiny or that "Playboy look." Everyone's makeup was perfect, not overdone, but instead put on the way makeup artists do, to play down any flaws and play up assets like full lips and model cheekbones. I wondered why there were not as many girls as our first night out and was told it was not a "required" night. It worked out for me because I actually had a place to sit this time. We pulled up to the Rainbow Bar and Grill. I had never been there, and as we entered, David Spade was sitting at one of the tables. This was clearly a happening place. Hef stopped to speak with David Spade for a moment, and then we were seated at our table. The bodyguards took pictures, and we ordered drinks, appetizers, and whatever we wanted from the pricey menu. Kelly and I were talking together, and Hef seemed to only talk to Deborah.

I raised my glass. "Hef, thanks for the dinner and having me join you."

All the unofficial girlfriends clinked glasses with mine. The girlfriends smirked and stared at me with disapproval. After we had eaten we were escorted across the way to the Roxy. There were a lot of paparazzi with large-lensed cameras, and Hef had us all line up next to the car and pose. The flashbulbs went off. Later I got to see myself and the group on "Celebrities Uncensored" #2 which was really cool (that airs on the E! network).

There were dozens of celebrities in the Roxy. Many of them came up to talk to Hef. I tried to look around discretely to see who was in the audience. Kelly started to name off many of those she could see without turning her head. I was star-struck. It was an invitation-only party, and we had the best seats in the house. Prior to the show starting, Marilyn Manson and Dita Von Teese came by to say hello to Hef. Of course, I got a picture of Marilyn Manson, Hef and Deborah in my picture. I was sitting across the table from them. Suddenly, Dita got very excited. I wondered what had happened. Kelly told me Hef had just told Dita she made the cover of *Playboy*. I was so excited I had gotten to meet her and hear the news at the same time she did.

During the show, all the dancers came by our table, and Christina Applegate even asked me a question as part of the show. I was the only audience member to be included in the show. Carmen Electra and Gwen Stefani were also part of the show. The performance was fabulous. Each of these famous women looked fantastic and played their part to the hilt.

After the show, we were escorted out by security guards and headed back to the mansion. I asked Kelly if they all went upstairs now. She shook her head. That was only Wednesdays and Fridays. Everyone went their separate ways, and when I returned to my room. I washed my face and climbed into bed but didn't sleep well. It had finally sunk in that my dream had probably come to an end. I had the choice of joining the group and having the time of my life. Going to the Grammy Awards, the Oscars, traveling, meeting celebrities, drinking Dom Perignon, great food, a great place to call home, money, cars, gifts were all within my grasp. I went over it all again and again all night. I thought about all the things I would never get to do—not to mention my ultimate goal of gracing the pages of *Playboy*. Would I risk my life—and my soul—for this lifestyle? I had come so far with the surgeries, the workouts, the planning, and the rejections to have the door so quickly closed.

Hef had given me the opportunity to make a choice—or did he? I realized I didn't have a choice, really. Either I had sex with him or I wouldn't succeed with *Playboy*. I was at the lowest point in my life. On the one hand, I wanted this so badly, but to even consider it made me disgusted with myself. I had even called Kelly and spoke to her about female condoms. She told me it wasn't allowed and if Hef discovered it he would be very offended. I tossed and turned. What was I thinking? Was I really considering this? I thought about the Prozac I took daily. Did this mean I wasn't happy with my man, my life, or my accomplishments? After all, it was only two minutes of sex twice a week. I'm basically an intelligent human being. I graduated in the top of my class with an extra tassel. Were the parties, fame, and perks I couldn't buy worth the price? I had a guy who loved me, I had my own business, and I owned my home. If I slept with him, and he didn't make me a girlfriend, like Michelle had mentioned, what then? I started making excuses for each event to try to come to a decision. There must have been hundreds of other girls without my advantages. I wondered how many had tried and failed. I wondered what had happened to them.

It was very late. I ordered some food from the kitchen and went to pick it up. One of the butlers came out with my order.

"You're older than the other girls. What are you? Twenty-five? Twenty-six?"

"Twenty-six . . . I thought you weren't supposed to talk to us." I snapped back at him for just even mentioning that I looked older then the other gals.

"Oh, I talk to most of you," he said. "It's just if Hef or one of the bodyguards comes in, I'll just say something about the food. Just so you know."

I finished my meal quickly and headed back. I didn't want to reveal too much. I woke up the next morning, Friday, feeling terrible because of my poor night's sleep. I was upset with myself for even considering selling myself out. My ultimate decision was a resounding NO. With that a huge weight was off my shoulders. I felt empowered and strong. Instead of getting angry that sex with Hef was my only option, the Prozac kicked in, and I decided I was going to get into the magazine without compromise. I was determined to prove it. I had to plan the next following days very carefully.

I had written Hef that I wanted to be with him. Now I was going to turn down the icon of sex. I thought long and hard about how I was going to do this without losing face, risking my life, my relationship with Bruce, and ultimately my soul. I needed to make the best of the situation I was presented with. I was one of few people who were staying at the mansion and partying with the man himself. I had to be a good sport and get through the rest of my visit unharmed. I had to make the girls not think I looked down at them or I would not be invited to even the large parties. I was having a great time and felt lucky to be part of the group without having to have sex with a seventy-six-year-old man to get into a magazine or have my bills paid. I told myself that the girls were using him as much as he was using them. They wanted to be in his magazine, live that life, get the perks and everyone comes out ahead. They knew what they were getting into.

Tonight was sex night, and I had started my period. A plan had suddenly arrived. This was the opportunity I needed to lead Hef on so that I didn't have to actually have sex with him but didn't turn him down either. My first visit upstairs was just nerves, this next time it was that time of the month, and the third time I'd be back home in Arizona.

From the bathroom I yelled, "Oh damn it! Shit!" I wanted Michelle to hear me. I came out of the bathroom talking loudly to myself. "I started my period! Now what am I going to wear? I was going to wear my white outfit. That's out of the question!" I hoped that my little drama had been heard and that Hef would be well-informed.

I did venture out and went to the game room in the mansion, played a few pinball machines, the kind they have at actual arcades, and took more pictures. I wandered through the enclosed zoo-like area where the birds were kept at night. Ponds of exotic and colorful fish and koi were dotted around the landscape. Lily pads floated, and small waterfalls burbled. It was peaceful. I watched koi swim lazily, sunlight gleaming off their shiny scales. I had brought my video camera and filmed some of the grounds, my room and other spots except the inside of the mansion. As I returned to the guest house, Michelle saw my camera and was hysterical.

"Are you crazy? If Hef hears about you taking pictures he would be very upset."

"Gee, I didn't know it wasn't allowed."

"No one saw you up by the offices did they?"

"I don't think so," I said. I wondered if this was a major problem. I knew I couldn't trust Michelle.

Later that evening the dinner buffet started. All of us went into the dining room, and many guests were already there. The buffet was a luxurious one, with prime rib and shrimp, and the types of selections you see at fancy hotels. All of the girlfriends had staked out their positions at Hef's table. I chose not to sit in the group area since there was not a place readily available. I sat with the cover girl for "Who wants to be a Playmate?" She was there because she had just finished shooting her Playmate video, photo, and came down with a terrible infection; too ill to travel. She said she was going out with us that night and was flying home the next day because she was finally feeling better. The guests were very old and personal friends of Hef's, I assumed. Not many young people were there but the girlfriends. After dinner Hef announced that it was "Movie Time," and all of us headed into the screening room. I had arrived late so there weren't many seats left and all the girlfriends had staked out their positions near Hef. I sat to the side—out of the "zone." They served bowls of popcorn. I asked if there was air-popped but they didn't respond.

It was just like you've read. Hef would read a little bit about the movie, and the crowd would laugh and seem entertained even though it was hard for me to understand what he was saying. I pretended to be very attentive. The movie started. Nothing special but a lot of people making a lot of noise that spoiled the film. After it was over, all of the girls returned to freshen up in our rooms and met back at the front lobby at ten o'clock for the night's events. The official pictures were taken before leaving. This time I was wearing lower heels, and I felt more comfortable. It started out just the same. The only thing different was this Friday the only girls that went were the eleven same girls who were naked upstairs Wednesday—no testing Playmates or other non-upstairs girls. When we got into the limo, Kelly informed me that a lot of times on the way back from the club things start to get a little wild in the limo.

"Like what?" I wanted to know.

"They start having sex with him. Tonight they'll probably start doing things on the way back."

Hef took pictures in the limo of all of us. He opened a bottle of Dom Perignon, and we headed out to the first club. We were escorted by the bodyguards, and Hef helped each of us out of the car one at a time. Everything was waiting for us—Evian and chilled glasses. The waitress took our order immediately. It was identical to Wednesday night —we danced with Hef, talked, and were escorted to and from the bathroom and surrounded by bodyguards. The girls didn't look around at the crowd. Hef was the center of attention. Once again it was amazing to walk into a place and have everything you wanted in an instant, to be catered to. This was the life Hef was used to since he founded *Playboy*.

I noticed that Kelly was talking a lot with the security guards. She finally returned to the table.

"What's up?"

"Tina Jordan Hef's ex-girlfriend's boyfriend is here and is staring down Hef. I noticed him out in the crowd, and I told the bodyguards."

"Oh, my God, this is so exciting!"

"It's not good. This isn't the first time he's followed Hef."

We were told we had to leave right away. There was a lot of commotion among the bodyguards and talking with Kelly. We headed out of the club, and Kelly was on the phone to someone to let him know we were on our way and to be prepared for our arrival. She put her head through the front window of the limo to talk to the two guys in the front seat. My heart was pounding with all the excitement and to think that I would be there if anything was to happen was incredible. The other club had an entire section set up for us and seemed happy to have us there. The owner was thankful to Kelly. He had no idea that we were all there because of a dangerous situation. We didn't stay long. I happened to be the last one on the way out. I saw Hef sitting in the couch area so I figured that I was supposed to wait. He seemed to have trouble getting up so I reached out to help him. He gave me a quick, hard look. I turned and headed toward the exit. I felt him put his hand on my back.

"Go." He gave me a large shove. His voice was brusque. Where was the smooth gentleman I had met so far?

I must have turned a dozen shades of red. He didn't speak to me the entire night—in the clubs, the limo, or the mansion. I got into the limo and sat by Kelly. She immediately knew something was wrong.

"Are you okay?"

I said, "Hef's really mad at me."

I told her what had happened. "Oh, my God, never, ever try to help him up."

She described a time that she tried to help him, and he yelled at her to never help him again. He didn't want anyone to ever think he was old or fragile. She told me not to worry about it. The ride back to the mansion was uneventful, and no one was saying much of anything. When we arrived I started to head back to my room. I admit I was disappointed. It was a very wild ride—quite a rush. Hard to believe it happened twice a week.

"Goodnight, Kelly."

"Where are you going?"

I said, "Well, I wasn't invited up, and it's that time of the month, anyhow."

She told me, "Once you have gone up and are out with us it's automatic that you come up. Don't be silly."

All the girls went through the front door of the mansion and up the winding staircase. Half the girls went to their rooms, and Kelly and I headed into the closet to retrieve our pink pajamas. I took off my clothes and the two of us got into the bathtub. This time Destiny got in as well. Hef came by with his camera and got us ready for our photo. Deborah wasn't in the tub, but Hef asked her to get in the picture so she crouched behind us and all four were in the photo. I got out, dried off, and slipped on my pajamas. I headed out to the main room and found a replica of Wednesday's evening. Loud techno music blared from speakers, porn was on the large screen, the girls had their vibrators and were topless. I took off my top but kept my pants on. This time Kelly, Destiny, and Melissa (aka China Doll) kept their bottoms on as well. Amber was wearing a bra and underwear and a couple of the other girls had their bottoms on, too.

Before anything began Amber said in a loud voice, "This is supposed to be a fucking orgy, not a topless party!" She apparently wasn't happy that many of us were not participating. I didn't like how aggressive she was. Hef lit up a rolled cigarette and passed it around. Deborah started to blow him and then had intercourse with him. She wiped him off for the next girl. Michelle went next, and Deborah wiped him off when they were finished. The girl-on-girl action was going on in the background with a repeat of the cheer "Fuck her, daddy, fuck her."

Suddenly one of the official girlfriends leaned into me. "Hey, new girl you're next."

"Oh, no, it's that time of the month."

She said, "You're new. He wants to fuck you, and he doesn't care."

One of the other official girlfriends was on top of Hef next. I don't think I had ever been so scared in my life. I was way at the end of the bed near Kelly.

"I'm terrified!" I told her under my breath.

"Follow my lead. Don't make eye contact. Pretend you are totally into me."

I realized that of the eleven girls that were up there, six of us had our pants on. Kelly looked scared and did try to shelter me. Hef came over anyway despite the rumored rule about leaving pants on. He moved in between the two of us. He reached his hands down my pants and under my underwear. I guessed he wanted to verify that I really did have my period. I didn't make eye contact, kept my head down and didn't say a word. Was I going to be raped? Held down? I didn't get the impression that he wasn't going to take "No" for an answer. It seemed like forever before he pulled his hand away. One of the girls that were wearing her bottoms began to give him a blow job to make amends for not enough girls having sex with him that night. She deep throated him, making extra noise. He had anal sex with Deborah, her arching her back and acting really into it, and that signaled the party was over and everyone disappeared into thin air.

I headed back to the guesthouse and came out of my room as Michelle finished showering.

"Not many participants tonight," I observed.

"Yeah and Hef is not happy."

I retreated to my room and called Bruce. I told him how scared I was, and he began to get very upset. He was worried about my welfare and whether I was going to be safe or not. I told him I would be fine. We talked for a long time. After we hung up, I ordered some food and went to pick it up. There were two girls in the main dining room playing Uno. I sat down to eat and chatted with them a bit. One of them was Hef's wife's best friend and lived with her across the street. I thought that it was pretty interesting that she could come over anytime she wanted. She was very nice and a former Playmate from many years ago. I joined them in their game and played for quite a while. Finally I said my goodbyes and went to bed.

It was Saturday morning and I was safe. I ate in the dining room alone. Two very large, mangy-looking dogs apparently had the run of the house and sat on my feet while I finished my meal. After I returned to my room, I decided to call Kelly. We gossiped about what had happened the night before. I actually told her a little bit about what Michelle and some of the other girls had hinted concerning her. I didn't quote Michelle because no one needed to hear such hurtful things. I told her that they were being mean to me for talking to her. She had noticed it as well. I didn't want to cause any problems for her or myself.

"They just don't like you because you're so nice. They don't realize that you're genuinely a good person and want to be part of their group. They must feel threatened by you."

I wasn't planning on returning, and I knew she really wanted to be in the group so I told her the things she could maybe change that wouldn't irritate them so much. We talked a while longer and then hung up. I ordered food again and began to eat it in the living room.

Like a shot, Michelle's daughter flew out of their bedroom. I asked her what was wrong. She moved her eyes up and motioned her head towards the bedroom she just came out of. I frowned. I didn't understand. She took me over to the very end of the living room and said very quietly that the camera light just came on. I wanted to know where it was. She said it was between the plants right above the closet in the middle. I wanted to know how she knew, and she told me she could see the red dot of light. I wanted to see this. She looked a little frightened but led me into the room and motioned with her eyes where I should look. She started showing me pictures of her mom to act like we were doing other things than looking for the camera. I sat on the bed for a moment and commented on how cozy a room it was. We left, and I told her that I didn't see it. She said he wasn't watching at the moment. She wanted to know if I had found the one in my room. I hadn't but asked her if she knew where it was. We couldn't locate it using the same ruse we had in her room.

I called Bruce and told him about the cameras. He wanted me out of there immediately. I told him I planned to leave a night early. I wasn't going to stay Sunday night and that as soon as the dinner and movie was over I would head back to the hotel where he was staying. I wanted to stay for the parties because there were going to be a lot of celebrities I would never have a chance to meet any other way. It was Fight Night. They had a buffet dinner similar to the night before except there were movie stars at this event. Verne Troyer ("Mini Me" from the Austin Powers movies) was there, and I had a picture taken with him. Bill Maher, Thora Birch, Scott Baio, Judd Nelson, and some of the other older movie stars were there. Lots of Playmates had driven up for the day. Lisa Dergan, Michael Bay (director of Pearl Harbor and others), Miss June—with whom I had hung out at the birthday party— and lots of others were there. I had pictures taken with everyone I recognized, and we all ended up in the screening room where there was a big fight to watch. Afterward everyone was wandering around. All the girls gathered for a picture as we had for the last three nights and then headed out to a large limo. We went to a different club and the night was very similar except for the fact that two other girls had joined us. After we got back to the mansion, I was told the following day was "fun in the sun day" and the festivities started at 2:00 p.m. I was exhausted and fell into bed.

The next day, Sunday, I headed out to the pool at the appointed hour. This pool was enormous, with a curving design and that lush California greenery around. Hef was already seated, playing backgammon with one of his friends. He was dressed in his trademark pajamas, and his main girlfriend was lounging in the chair positioned very close to him. All the official girlfriends seemed to have a certain order and positioned themselves in an array around Hef. I walked by him and nodded my head in greeting. I sat by Michelle and her daughter up on the grass. She had brought her dog. Many new girls I didn't recognize were in chairs by the pool. Kelly showed up and situated herself next to me. Her friend, Susan, who was a Sunday-guest, joined us. Michelle looked very annoyed that we had joined her.

I said quietly to Kelly, "We should move."

"No. You picked the perfect spot next to Michelle. You want to stay in good contact with one of his girlfriends so that it appears you fit in."

I thought, fitting in with what? I didn't have sex with him. I just sat there because all of the recliners were spoken for, and I loved playing with Michelle's dog because I missed mine. More people drifted in to play backgammon with Hef. He was completely immersed in the game and there was no talking the entire Fun-In-The-Sun-Day, other than a few quick kisses from girls who were late or were new to the Sunday events. Hef didn't talk to any of the girls. Two butlers were taking orders from the special Sunday menu. They were also photographers, and they took pictures of any girls doing something memorable. Kelly told me that if we wanted to get into the front of the magazine "Hanging with Hef" we had to flash and Fun-In-The-Sun-Day was the best time to do it. Okay, I thought. We took off our bathing suit tops and started rubbing oil on each other. We were perfectly positioned in Hef's line of sight, able to distract him. It worked. He stood up and called for one of the men to start taking pictures. The main girlfriends were glaring at us. This was the only moment that Hef moved away from his game. We were proud of ourselves. Two other girls joined us, Destiny and Susan, and we all posed topless for the cameraman. Afterward I looked over and one of Hef's sons was watching us. Then I felt horribly embarrassed. To top it off the other girl's son was swimming in the pool keenly interested in the action.

"I'm surprised they let the kids out by the pool area on Sunday's," I said to Michelle.

She shrugged. "They're used to it. They don't care."

I looked around. Many of the girls were topless in the lounge chairs. I was shocked to see them uncovered. One girlfriend had stretch marks marring her breasts and was lying there naked. I was surprised that she would dare to lay out undressed. Otherwise the Sunday was very tame and unexciting. A few of the girls went down to the gym to work out and use the tanning beds. Kelly and I went out to the aviary and took pictures of ourselves with the monkeys, birds, and flamingos.

When the afternoon drew to a close I went back to my room to start all over again. Buffet dinner and a movie were going to begin shortly. I called Bruce. My rock was not so rock-like at this point. He insisted I come home. Over the last few days he had said so many wonderful, supportive, and loving things to me. He had told me how much he loved me, how special I was, how proud he was, and how great my morals were. He missed me. He was lonely. I felt much loved and told him I would leave after the buffet and not stay for the movie. This seemed to relieve him. We hung up, and I started to redo my makeup for the night's events.

The buffet was served outdoors. Mostly the same older people who attended the Friday night Fight Night were there. No celebrities; mostly just old friends and Hef's current, and aspiring to be, girlfriends. I helped myself to more food than I normally would have since my figure wasn't going to matter so much the next day. The desserts were wonderful—chocolate mousse, éclairs, pies and cakes and beautiful as any you see at a high-class bakery. I waited at the buffet area to tell Hef I was going to be leaving early.

I followed him to the pool bar and approached him slowly. "Hef, I'm leaving and just wanted to thank you for having me here."

"Okay, dear. Wait right here a moment." He headed back to the mansion.

I waited a little while and when he returned he handed me a stack of photographs.

I was so surprised. "Thank you so much!"

He looked at the bartender and asked him to take a picture of the two of us. I smiled and said, "Thanks, Hef." I headed back to my room. I had already packed. I told the valet that I was leaving and turned my key into the security room, and he helped me get out to my car. I drove out the back exit of the Playboy Mansion and watched it disappear from my rearview mirror. I headed to the casino and Bruce.

When I arrived, he was waiting for me out front. It made me feel good to see him, especially outside watching for me. The valet took my car and helped unload my luggage. Bruce didn't seem glad to see me. I was puzzled and disappointed not to have been greeted with more enthusiasm. He did not even give me a hug, a hello, nothing, there was just silence. We went up to the room, and he wanted to be intimate right away. I was pretty turned off with the way he had met me though I had been looking forward to sex when I had seen him standing out in front of the hotel. I told him how I felt. We talked for a long time, and it all worked out. I realized it was realistic for him to feel out of sorts over my stay at the mansion, and he realized that in my heart, I was still the same Jill Ann I always was.

We went back to Arizona, and I had to tell my mother and grandma the story about what goes on in the Playboy Mansion. All I ended up saying was, "They have sex with him, Mom—and all at the same time" I couldn't say much else, because my grandfather being in the room and I had to whisper what I did say as it was.

"So? What did you expect? What happened?" My Mom was surprised that I thought it would be any different. "Only twelve girls get chosen. They have to stand out to get picked." She seemed surprised that I thought it would be different and seemed to wonder why I did not stay. She knew how much I had wanted to be in *Playboy*—and she wanted it at my age.

"Mom, they don't use any protection!"

"Oh, my God. Really? In this day and age with so many diseases? Well, I can understand why you didn't stay."

That was the extent of our conversation. My grandma told my grandpa that those girls probably have to have sex with Hefner to get into the magazine. She let Grandpa think she was guessing even though she knew the truth from me.

"Oh, Hugh Hefner has so many women there at the mansion they probably have sex all the time. He probably has orgies—just him and a whole bunch of girls."

My grandpa replied, "No, he does not have orgies. That's not how they get into the magazine. How ridiculous! What an imagination!"

Actually, I couldn't have even imagined or thought up just how strange and treacherous it could be at the mansion.

Chapter Seven

I survived the mansion and very plainly had been exposed to the casting couch of L.A. I was angry, didn't know if I was going to do anything about it, expose it or just scream. On Prozac, the whole situation seemed to nudge me toward a positive frame of mind. I was challenged and determined to get into *Playboy* without having to sleep with anyone. A normal woman would perhaps have given up. I was going to make the magazine want me. I still held a grip on my dream.

Kelly was the only connection to the *Playboy* mansion that I had, so I called her a lot after I got back to discuss what had happened and what had gone on. Within the next week, Kelly was no longer going to be invited out on Wednesdays and Fridays, but that she could still come up to the parties and Sundays. She felt she had been kicked out for several reasons: not having sex with Hef the last time, bossing Amber around, not getting me to sleep with Hef and lots of little other things. Since she was no longer part of the group, she had no reservations about speaking her mind. She was devastated, to say the least, but she tried to convince herself that it was a good thing. It was terribly dangerous to have unprotected sex. She revealed to me that she had done girl-on-girl films to put herself through college. She was worried that she might have any number of diseases after these escapades with Hef. She decided she was going to have herself checked out. I thought it a little late in the game but a good idea nonetheless. We talked about many other things. One point I distinctly remember was that the time she shepherded me upstairs that first time she had no idea I had not only never been upstairs before but I had never been at the mansion before. I went to a dream visit to the mansion and wound up in a full-blown orgy. Welcome to L.A.!

* * * *

After I left the mansion, I kept in touch with Kelly. I was amazed at the amount of intrigue that went on. I had seen some of it, of course, but I was still to learn much, *much* more. One night on the phone, Kelly asked, "Have you heard from anybody from the mansion?"

"No, nothing at all. Not from anybody," I replied.

Kelly then told me that because of some back-stabbing and gossiping, Hef had actually "canned" two girls—including her. In Kelly's case, she was the victim—just as I had been on the hairstyling trip with Michelle. After Kelly found out that she was no longer going to be invited to the mansion she had this to say: "No, but it is a good thing, I don't want to be. I get to go to the parties, and I get to go on Sundays, and I can walk around and socialize and find a husband . . . but then I don't have to do the orgy thing you know and that is really good. But yeah the phones were definitely tapped everything was filmed, yes definitely."

She went on, "I could make Playmate if I wanted to. I could be a girl-friend if I wanted to—and they saw the competition coming."

The treachery was so extensive. Kelly said that Hef would whisper to her to do things for him on the side. Then Mary would call her on a Tuesday to go out that Wednesday. Even though Hef would tell her on Sunday "See you on Wednesday," Mary would always call her on Tuesday for a head count for the limo.

I asked Kelly how she ended up getting into *Playboy*, and she said she was in Las Palmas and Hef found her—and she had been there ever since. July was the anniversary when she and Hef met. She is still allowed to go up every Sunday and parties.

* * * *

Both Sarah and Destiny, a few days after my departure, were made official girlfriends. Hef took Sarah and Destiny at separate times into his bed-room, and he has a safe in this room where he keeps the diamond *Playboy* Platinum necklaces, and he presented them to each girl individually meaning that they are now official girlfriends. Kelly said this is why the girls were freaking the night I was out with all of them and was wearing that long dia-mond necklace that night because it was exactly like it. Even though Michelle said I would never be a girlfriend and that Destiny was just brought up their for sex only, days later she became an official girlfriend.

After Hef gave both the girls official girlfriend necklaces the tension was extremely high in the limo this night according to Kelly. This night Britney, who later became Miss January, was already campaigning for Playmate of the year® even though she just had shot her centerfold not for this year but for the next year, so the tension was insane. The girls were so mean to her because she shot her centerfold, and all the girls want to be Playmates, and she is going to be a big major playmate.

I asked Kelly if the exact thing happens every Wednesday and Friday, and she said yes, that was a ritual. Kelly said she had to write Amber an apology because she was really mad because Kelly was bossing her around at the orgy. She said that she was just trying to help me relax and joked, "It's just like you can't please everybody."

Kelly said that the girls thought that she took me upstairs on her own, and they were all mad at her for that.

Kelly said, "They think that I took you upstairs on my own, and they don't know that Hef asked me to do it. He doesn't want to upset his girl-friends because they just think I took you up there on my own."

She added that one of the girls who drives up on Sundays, "A girlfriend was telling everyone that Hef called me at home and told me I was canned. She said, 'Hef would never do that. He is too sweet. He would have a lady do it, but he wouldn't have himself do it,'" Kelly defended him.

I asked Kelly if the girls were upset with me and if I shouldn't have gone upstairs. She said that she didn't think they were mad at me, but she didn't think they liked the competition. "I think that you were a huge threat to them, you know, and they don't like Hef's attention to go anywhere else. They all have no real security."

"Well, it is hard enough to share him with seven people as it is."

"Yeah, but you had a better body then any of them. You could be a centerfold. . . . It was like damn they were going to hate you right off the bat." She said that Amber, Destiny, Deborah and the other girls openly say they want to be Playmates. She said the twins are what started the whole thing— they were major girlfriends.

Kelly went on. "Everyone has had their turn upstairs. You have to have sex with Hef or the girls don't like you. They get mad or angry at the girls that don't have sex because they have to do it more. They told me that I would have been a girlfriend if I would have kept having sex with Hef. I guess this is true, but they just want someone else to do the work so what can you do? I give up, it was like 8th grade, it wasn't even that . . . it was 2nd grade."

I couldn't believe they were so threatened by me. What about the Play-mates on the videos of parties who look like they're having so much fun to-gether?

Kelly said, "They're not threatened by Nicole, Destiny, or Sarah. Anyone who is a threat to them this is when the problems come in."

Pictures shot 2003 for my Zed Card to get bookings
for Gordon Raels Agency.

She said if you write Hef a personal letter he is the only one that gets it. She said if you send him a gift bag he is the only one that gets it. She said her girlfriend Susan wants to be a girlfriend so bad and that is her goal in life. She comes up on Sundays. She told Susan to get a boob job and dye her hair. She said that the girls are so threatened by her because she is bi-sexual . . . and the others aren't bisexual and they must pretend. I told her that I did not understand why that none of the girls acted like they had a good time up there.

"Why? Because if you don't have sex with him you're cut! I think about girls other than you at other times that didn't have sex with him, and they weren't invited back up there. You have to have sex with Hef—that is the rule."

I felt badly for Kelly. She said she really didn't have fun going out Wednesdays and Fridays. "I don't enjoy it because you are roped off. You can't talk to any of the guys. Like at the big parties if you are one of the girlfriends you cannot leave that table. You can't go up to Mathew Perry, you can't go up to Luke Wilson, and if you are not a girlfriend you can do whatever you want. There are so many girls that come and go, and who knows who will last there? Michelle is a really good fuck . . . she is a great fuck . . . She is a really good fuck . . . she really can work it . . . she has an amazing body and she is a really good fuck and that's what's important." She said this out of the blue, I guess she was trying to decide on her performance of a reason she got cut.

"Not to be negative, Kelly, but you gave Hef a blow job. What could you catch from that?"

"I am sure you can get gonorrhea of the throat, but I think if one of the girls had it that they would all know, and we would all have it by now."

We started talking about getting on the permanent party list and she said everyone sends flowers, candy and he doesn't remember these things. She gives him disposable cameras because he is always taking pictures. She said a girl named Stephanie goes up on Sundays and has been for four years, and they call her every week to invite her up. She says Mary or Joyce are the only ones that really make the calls to the girls.

We continued talking about the girls, and Kelly said that the girlfriends don't talk to Britney, and they don't talk to Destiny.

"I wonder now that she got her necklace, though," I mused aloud.

"Nope! Everybody doesn't like anybody . . . that's just how it is."

"It is so sad that they just don't all get along and have a great time together."

"No, they all say he is an old geezer and that he is going to die. They all think they are going to get a million dollars, and they're not. They all want to

go to the beauty shop, they want the money, they want the clothes, and they want the cars and they're all fighting for it. They all want a new Porsche; they all want a new Cadillac like Deborah's. I am not cliquey at all. I don't like gossip, I don't put up with it, and I don't put up with people disrespecting Hef, and I'll snap at them if they disrespect Hef in anyway. So of course they are not going to like me. Of course, you know I lost my thing . . . whatever . . . . my gig."

Kelly really seemed to have a lot of insight into Hef. She said that Hef actually reads all of the jokes that are sent in to the magazine, that she sees him reading them. That he loves the jokes and gets off on them, and he thinks it's fun. She said that he does not as much now since he had a stroke . . . that he is supposed to go slow. She said her dad couldn't have sex with ten girls and he was ten years younger then Hef!

She said when Tina Jordan was the boss that things were a lot different. "But then Tina made Playmate, and as soon as she did she was like 'Bye-bye' . . . 'See ya'"

I asked her who lived there vs. who had to travel in for parties, and she said the following. Sarah drives up, Destiny drives up, Michelle stays in the guest house Wednesday through Sunday, and Jennifer drives up and stays in the main house Wednesday through Sunday. Deborah, Amber, Amanda, and Nicole live there every day.

* * *

More conversation with Kelly . . .

"I'll tell you who moved in! China Doll—and she got a dog."   Kelly said,
"But Hef always acted like he had only seven girlfriends."

"Oh, no . . . there were nine and twelve and eleven." Apparently, it fluctuates.

I told Kelly what Michelle had said that I could sleep with Hef and I still would never be a girlfriend.

"What a bitchy thing to say!"

"Michelle said I would just go home broken-hearted and I might end up with some disease, and no matter what he has his seven girlfriends and that's it. I started the conversation that I did not want to be a girlfriend and that is what she responded to my comment. I told her I did not want to be a girl-friend so I wanted to let her know because I did not want the girls not to like me and that I just wanted to have a really good time there the few days that I was going to be there. I didn't want them to feel threatened or anything."

"Yeah." Kelly responded.

Kelly was talking to one girl who used to be a girlfriend and she said every time she slept with him she would get a yeast infection and that herpes was going around and that she didn't live there anymore. She lived there for seven months. She was a Playmate and stuff. She said ever since she moved out she hasn't had a problem, but when she lived there every week her health was so bad she would be doubled over in pain and they would have to leave parties because of her yeast infections and her UTIs. She said between that and the herpes she was always sick."

We discussed what Michelle had said about Hef only having seven official girlfriends and that they were already chosen and Kelly—never one to hide her opinion, joked, "She was talking out of her ass. Yes, he has different girlfriends. Britney lives in San Antonio Texas and just flew in and she is a girlfriend so he has more than seven girlfriends. That was just a big fat lie because she was just threatened by you."

Kelly did say that you don't become a girlfriend and then leave and come back. This is what the Playmate that lived there for seven months told her. That you just get one shot and if you blow it you blow it. In Kelly's case she said one girl was responsible for getting her kicked out. She said that that could have been how she got kicked out just from bossing Amber around. She said Amber was the one that got the other girl kicked out.

I couldn't imagine the pressure. "How you could live under that kind of circumstance where you just said something wrong you would be kicked out?"

Kelly said the only reason Amber had not moved out was because she hadn't made Playmate. The Playmate that got thrown out of the mansion by Amber said that Deborah is bulimic and that is how she stays so skinny. The cat fighting was incredible!

I told her I figured Hef would change his mind and call her back up to go out on Wednesdays and Fridays. She said that if he didn't it was fine with her because it really is nice not having a yeast infection. "

"I am really glad I'm out. You know . . . do you remember when I filled up the bathtub with bubbles? Then I took over someone else's job of filling up the bath tub with bubbles and that was Destiny's first time up there too. Apparently, doing this other person's job was threatening to her." I knew she was speaking about Deborah.

Kelly also believed there was a quota of sorts of gals that they had to put in the magazine for color reasons. "Miss June was only chosen for quota and so is China Doll. I can't tell you about another one . . . that's under a gag order. But they would say, 'We needed a dark-haired dark-eyed girl who is kind of Latina.'"

The other girls also tried to stop her from telling Hef that she wanted to be a Playmate. She told Mary (one of Hef's employees who has been an employee for years) and she said, "Fuck them. Go right on in and tell him." So she did test for Playmate, and she just did it a short time ago.

I said it sounds like if he wants you to be a Playmate—and he's the one who can make you one. She agreed and said did you know that his main girlfriend Tina Jordan tested for Playmate three times before she made it. Jennifer tried out for Playmate, and they ended up putting her as a cyber girl. Amber tried out, and they put her as cyber girl. He offered Deborah cyber girl as well, and she turned it down. We then started talking about large events, and she said only the official girlfriends got to go to main events like the AFI awards. One of the secretaries called Destiny at the last moment since she became an official girlfriend and told her we know this is short notice but Hef wants you to go to the AFI awards. So Destiny ran all over town trying to find an evening gown.

I told Kelly that I had just got back from Vegas and was showing one of the casino guest relations hosts my pictures out with Hef, and the young casino host got all excited and pointed to Destiny's picture and said that's "Paris."

I told him "No, that's Destiny."

He said, "No. That's Paris. She works at Spearmint Rhino in California." Destiny is probably her real name; Paris is probably her stage name.

Kelly said "I can neither confirm nor deny anything about her, but I have known who she is the entire time, but I am such a good secret keeper."

"I can't believe it is such a small world. I was up in the Diamond VIP room at Rio Hotel in Vegas and the employee there knew her."

Kelly started laughing and said, "But I have the shit on her. If they ever knew, but man, she is so sweet I would never bust her I would never betray her I would never tell." We started talking about the necklace that I wore that was so much like the one that Hef gives them and she said "they freaked."

I told her that I felt bad wearing the necklace and making them have added pressure. It's not in me to play mind games with people.

"Don't feel bad, Jill Ann. They are miserable people. They're sad and miserable. You know it's got to be rough to live there. You have a 9:30 curfew, you can't date other guys, it is very hard to sneak out."

I interrupted and said, "You know Destiny has a regular boyfriend."

"Like I said I can neither confirm nor deny."

"She told me about her boyfriend, and I told her that I thought that was cool that Hef didn't mind you having other boyfriends."

"I don't think she tells him. Hell, I wouldn't tell people I was having sex with Hugh Hefner."

"You know, I was surprised that they didn't have me like sign something, you know when I went upstairs . . . like a confidentiality agreement. I guess he doesn't care."

She said, "I have seen strangers go up there like Britney they brought her home from the bar one night. They picked her up at a bar one night, and she went home and had sex with him. You know so it's like he has no fear of AIDS."

"Do you think it's because he is older?"

"Yeah, I think he would rather die younger than at 102. He doesn't want to make it to a decrepit age, so he is not afraid to die lonely, and they would cover it up so well. You know, the most recent AFI award was for Tom Hanks. And I heard Tom was going to play Hugh Hefner in a movie. That is why Hef wanted to go to hang out with Tom Hanks now. Can you imagine the nicest guy in Hollywood playing Hugh Hefner? That just cracks me up. Hef is just waiting for a script, and he has selected Tom Hanks to play him but there is no script yet though."

We talked some more, and Kelly insisted that Hef wants harmony amongst the girls. He doesn't like conflict. "It used to be really nice last year. There was a whole different set of girls except for Amber, who is the only one from the prior group. The girls used to be really, really, really nice, and then they all left once they made Playmate."

"I wonder if once he shares them with the world in the magazine and then he doesn't want them anymore? What do you think?"

"No, no, no. They leave on their own. Once they make Playmate, they leave. He is learning that once they make Playmate they bolt because Dalene lived there, Tina Jordan lived there, and as soon as they made Playmate they left. I think he is learning to get less attractive women who would never make Playmate to live there so that no one leaves him. The last set of girls were not so back fighting, cat fighting whatever. The girls that are there just think they are the shit and it's just not fun. Tina Jordan was best friends, with Michelle for years and she is the one that got Michelle in. At least it is good for Michelle's daughter because they eat well, you know. It's a pretty good life. They act like it is prison, but you get to tan, eat, work out, I don't know what they are bitching about. They were all like 'oh we have to do that thing on Friday.' They all dread it."

"Crazy . . . You know, I was wondering . . . How did you know you were cut?"

"They don't call or tell you or anything. It's just that they always just call you to invite you and when I didn't get the phone call I knew I was cut."

* * * *

The next party was coming up. July 4th. Kelly was very excited to go. I told her I hadn't been invited.

"What? Why not?"

"I don't know. I think it's because I didn't have sex with Hef. I'm afraid I won't ever be invited back."

She said, "Write him a letter and mention that you weren't invited. There's not a lot of time so you need to get on it right away."

I decided to call Jenny who spearheads the lists for all events and told her I hadn't been called for the Fourth of July party.

She checked and said, "Yep. You're not on it."

"Why?"

"I don't know." She was very blunt.

"Is it because of my visit to the mansion?"

"I couldn't tell you, but the list has already been finalized."

"Can I be added?" I asked.

"Hef is the only one who could add your name."

"Can you ask Hef if I can go?" I wondered.

She said, "I wouldn't if I were you. Try for the Midsummer Night party. That's the next one."

"When should I ask about this?"

She said, "Right away. The lists are made far in advance, but I wouldn't buy an outfit if I were you."

"So does this mean you already know he will say no?"

She hesitated and then replied, "No . . . I just say that to everyone"

I thanked her and hung up. I was upset and thoroughly dejected. Besides not being in the magazine, now I was no longer going to be invited to the parties. I had to figure out something. I didn't know how to plead my case to go to the parties and still get in the magazine. I was going to have to write a masterpiece letter. I included one of the pictures of me, Hef's main girlfriend, and two other girls in the tub. I put it in a beautiful silver frame that could hold several and included several of the pictures I had taken during my stay. I sent it June 22nd.

Dear Hef,

I just wanted to thank you for having me to your home and to be part of your life for those days. It was an honor. I just have to say you are the man!

You are the true *Playboy*! Wow! What a party. You are living every man's dream. That was the most erotic nights of my life. The whole experience was a dream come true. Every night was wonderful and a blast. I had never been with a girl before or even had one touch me until that night. I have only been with a handful of guys sexually. I just got my ears and belly pierced about four months ago and the strongest substance that has been in my body is alcohol. I have never smoked anything. I am confident with my body because I work hard keeping it in great shape (treadmill, weights, etc.—all for *Playboy*). The only time anyone other than a boyfriend has seen me undressed was for you and my submissions to *Playboy*. Here are the pictures I promised. I fell in love with *Playboy* when I was a young girl. Later on, in 1995, I began collecting autographed covers of *Playboy* magazine. The first one was Drew Barrymore. The collection is very large now as you can see from the pictures. I just wanted you to know what a big fan I am. Any parties, events, or clubbing where you need another blonde I'll be on the next plane. I travel to L.A. many times a year. I'll pay my own way and get to the mansion on my own. Please, Hef let me come to the Midsummer Night party. I had such an awesome time at your birthday party. I already have an outfit designed in the hopes I will get to come. Please, please, please!

P.S. Please consider doing a small pictorial and poker article on me in your magazine. Playboy.com gaming division is talking about going online with Holdem poker. That is my best game and what I am most famous for. It would help pub *Playboy* gaming on the map for the poker world, and it would let me be part of *Playboy* history. I am really good at live poker and poker tournaments. I take poker very seriously – 90 percent of poker players are men and they all would buy this magazine with me in it. They all know me! I would also get Poker Digest or Card Player to run an article about it coming out so everyone would know what issue. I signed tons of Poker Digest covers when it came out and it was the best time. I just loved it. Poker is a nationwide sport that is so popular now that it is getting widespread publicity. Let me just be a part of *Playboy* magazine. I need more *Playboy* to make my life complete!

At the same time I sent this I sent gifts to the official girlfriends all in the same box so that he would be able to read the letter and see what I was giving the girls.

To Deborah, Amber, Amanda, Jennifer, Nicole, Sarah, and Michelle,

Thanks for making my stay at the mansion so terrific. I had the best time going clubbing with all of you. Go Lakers! I got seven differently styled shirts for you all so that you wouldn't have the same ones. I also made this pink cotton candy exfoliating body polish for all of you. Hope you like it. All of you are so beautiful and nice!

I received a very short letter from Hef on July 1st: It contained that I would be on the Midsummer Night's Dream list.

I noticed the change in tone right away in that he didn't sign off with "love" and was a little taken back at the formal "sincerely." I guess my status had been downgraded. I hadn't mentioned the July party based on my conversation with Jenny, but I was excited that I was back on the list. All had not been lost. I would really have been flipped out if I hadn't been invited because of my lack of sexual participation. Kelly went to the July party, and she said she had a terrific time.

My invitation to the August 3rd party arrived July 11th. Countless e-mails back and forth with *Playboy* Casino seemed positive, but as of the end of July nothing had come of it.

The day arrived for the big party. I flew in that day and out the next. Kelly picked me up at the airport, and we drove directly to the party. I knew that cameras were not allowed. Only Hef's girlfriends and the hired photographers had them. Of course, that didn't stop most people, and I sneaked mine in this time—I'd of course seen people at the first party with them and knew if I didn't get caught, it would be okay. I got pictures with Marilyn Manson and Dita Von Tesse, both of whom were very nice. Leo DiCaprio wouldn't let me get a picture of him. He said, "Maybe later." Kelly noticed Britney Spears sitting at a table talking with a girl while her very large and imposing bodyguard stood in front to control anyone coming up to her. I asked him if I could speak to Britney.

He told me, "Give her a minute."

I was the only one waiting and the only one that seemed to want to meet her. All the other party goers either didn't see her or were too shy to come up. It seemed that I waited an eternity as I watched her talk to her friend. As soon as she was through with her conversation, I stepped forward quickly and started to speak to her. She pulled down her hat to cover her face and got up to leave.

"You're even prettier in person," I said. She didn't acknowledge me at all. I asked Jamie Foxx for permission to take a picture and told him that his jokes about the Playboy Mansion were wonderful. He didn't respond at all and walked away after the photo was shot. I was striking out. I suddenly noticed Simon Cowell out in the smoking area and asked him. Another girl and I who had almost the same outfit as mine wanted a picture of the three of us. He seemed really nice compared to the show until my friend handed her camera to someone to take the picture. The first picture with my camera was fine. She couldn't figure out to run her digital camera for the second one. He flipped out. "Oh, come on!" He rolled his eyes and walked off.

People were dressed in a wide array of party wear and costumes that tried to fit with the theme. I wore angel wings. Other girls had lots of glitter in their hair and on their cheeks. Some wore outfits that seemed to invoke the fairytale land of Shakespeare's play.

As we were leaving the party, we noticed Leo DiCaprio and Tobey Maguire waiting for their limo while the rest of us were loading on the shuttle bus to return us to the pickup point at UCLA. This was my chance to get a picture with them. Kelly refused to take the picture so when he said it was okay I handed the camera to one of his friends. I stood between them. Leo was squeezing my shoulder so hard it hurt. The flash went off and their limo pulled up. Leo asked me if I wanted to join them, but I couldn't of course. I was thrilled at the invitation. That wasn't my style, but I will admit that at that moment I wished it were.

At the airport I met a girl who had gone to the party.

"Were you at Midsummer Night's Dream last night?" she asked. I nodded. I think she based that assumption on my breasts, platinum blonde hair, and the wings I was carrying that were part of my outfit. We sat together on the plane, and we hit it off right away with our *Playboy* connection. I mentioned that I had gotten to party with Hef and stay at the mansion.

"I'm going to write Hef a letter and tell him that I want to become a girl-friend."

I gave her a strange look and said, "They're intimate with him. I found out the hard way so if you're not prepared to sleep with him, don't write the letter."

She shrugged. "I'm willing. Tell me about your visit."

"Unfortunately, I signed a confidentiality agreement so I really can't talk about it." I hadn't signed any such thing, but I didn't want to tell someone about my experience if it was going to jeopardize my being invited to future parties or getting into the magazine.

She said, "I made Cyber Girl. My pictorial's coming out soon."

"That's great!" I said. "How about I throw you a party? We can round up a bunch of girls, get a limo and go to a club to celebrate."

We became better friends, and I did throw the promised party. We had a huge twenty-two passenger Lincoln Navigator and since she had only a few girlfriends I brought many of mine to ensure the best turnout. I did eventually reveal the story of my visit, and she decided not the write the letter to Hef about becoming a girlfriend. The unprotected sex information really floored her and I believe that was the deciding factor changing her mind. She told me many stories of what she had encountered. Apparently, it was the same in Chicago's *Playboy* department with the person that ultimately made her Cyber Girl. This really brought us together, and we had something to complain about to each other. She read all of my correspondence with Hef so she wouldn't make the same mistake I had. I wanted her to know that it was not a game and if she was not willing to go through with it, she had better be careful because he wasn't kidding or flirting. He was serious.

I decided to write a thank you to Hef for the party as well as dig myself out of the hole I felt I was in. I had submitted my pictures to Jeff Cohen for Special Editions and received a rejection letter. I really felt that I had what it took for *Special Edition's Especially Voluptuous Vixens*. There must have been a flag on my name with *Playboy* and that was why I hadn't been chosen.

Dear Hef,

I just wanted to say thank you for having me to the party. It was the best. Anyhow, in reference to my last trip, I had every intention of staying at the mansion. I had all my loose ends tied up and didn't plan to come home for many months! You could probably tell by how many clothes I brought and the new extra blonde color you like. I must confess I didn't realize that you slept with all of the girls; especially all at once. I thought maybe one of two were your main girlfriends and the rest were for show or occasional. Please don't hold it against me that I was naïve. I am so sorry. I wasn't trying to be a tease. I have never had sex with anyone without getting to know him well and dated awhile. I know "if you don't swing, don't ring"—but I thought it part of the promotional idea. I guess I thought I would move into the mansion and get to play dress up and hang out—be one of your girlfriends. To tell you the truth, I think about it every day. I was turned on and wanted to join in. I was horny as ever presented with a bed full of beautiful women and the icon of the world. The emotional risk of not feeling good about myself was too high. You always say in your interviews "once a friend always a friend." How can I be this friend? I want so much to be a part of your life, your company, even if it is only parties, Sundays—whatever you can give. I can offer in return to tell everyone that I meet how wonderful you are and how much I love *Playboy* and promise to do my sit-ups and work out to keep the *Playboy* body as the vision that is in my mind. Please take this bed as a thank you and have fun with it. It's brand new and never used, especially for you and your girlfriends.

With love,

Jill Ann

P.S. Please let me come to the Halloween Party!

The bed mentioned was a $200 bondage bed that I purchased at a sex store to spice up Bruce and my sex life. It had been sitting in the closet for a few years, and I never even took it out of the box. I decided that Hef was the perfect person to give it to, get it out of my house and even gain a few brownie points.

On September 16, 2002 I received a letter back from Hef. It basically said that he understood that "perhaps" there had been some "misunderstanding" between us, but he didn't feel either of us suffered any for the weekend and there were no hard feelings.

I noticed the closing right away even before I read the letter. I was relieved. It was warmer than the last time. He didn't mention the gift. I wondered if he didn't like it or if someone intercepted it before giving him the letter. It was a positive letter in my view and maybe indicated I would be taken off the "Do Not Use Jill Ann Spaulding" list for *Playboy*.

During the Midsummer party a guy had approached me and I was rude, reluctantly, because of my experiences with other men who had come up to me.

"You are by far the most beautiful woman at this party."

"That is so sweet," I said. "I'll bet you say that to all the girls."

He said, "Actually I haven't." He handed me his card, and it had the *Playboy* logo. Gordon Rael, Talent Consultant to Playmate Promotions/Playboy Model Agency.

"This is the only card I've given out the entire night. Please don't show it to anyone else at the party. I'm not interested in anyone else. Send me your head shot and some pictures in the mail as soon as you can."

He came back over to me later that night when I was standing alone in the food line, came up behind me and whispered, "You really are unbelievably beautiful. I must represent you. You have to call my office."

I smiled at him without saying anything, and he walked away. Because he didn't press me much I decided that maybe he was legit and this might be a great new lead. On August 13th he emailed me. I hadn't sent the pictures to him at that point because I was waiting to have some 8 by 10's printed. He wanted to know if I remembered him. He wanted to get in touch. I don't remember what I wrote back, but I do remember telling him I would get the pictures to him right away. He phoned me a few days after they arrived. The pictures were terrific, he said, and he wondered when I was coming to Los Angeles. I decided to call him back a few days later and I recorded the conversation. I wanted to make sure I had not forgotten anything or misunderstood any of his representations.

Gordon Rael Audio Tape

INTRODUCTION: G: Gordon Rael
                    J: Jill

J: Do you remember me? I showed you the pictures and you called me last night?

G: Sure, yeah, I remember you.

J: I feel bad, because I was driving down the road and we had just buried our aunt…and it was, like a bad day.

G: That's a drag. Don't worry about it. I understand.

J: The main thing I want from *Playboy* is that I'm a professional poker player.

G: Okay, I don't t really deal with *Playboy* stuff.

J: Not really?

G: Not at all.

J: How did you get that card so Playboyish?

G: Because I'm a consultant for *Playboy*. I make their deals.

J: So you can't…

G: That's what I do. I can get any girl I want in as a Playmate, and I do their deals and when a girl is done with her month they come to me to be their agent.

J: Wow.

G: That's my situation with *Playboy*, and I help them with anything they need me for. And, ah… if someone comes up to me and says, "I want to be a Playmate" and she is very, very good, then I make it happen. And, if someone is good and wants to be a pictorial, like this month, Jordan, and…you know, I found her. Dalene is Playmate of the year®, I found her. Um…that's why my office is at *Playboy* because I represent all the Playmates.

J: I want to do that.

G: And, I also do TV and films and commercials.

J: Right, which I would like to do after that.

G: Yeah, you know the Playmates like to do um….for instance I have those — ads that you see in the movie *What Women Want* that was in Mel Gibson's office. I do those ads and I do the ones, the pin-up type, Cutty Shark and Tanqueray and all that. And then I do Frederick's and all those type of things, but um….what I do is um…you know in promotions, whenever there is a deal to be done, I'm the one that does it. Hold on one quick second.

J: Sure.

(Pause)

G: So, that's my story, so I mean….so I've gotten about eighteen girls in the centerfold.

J: Wow. How can I? Um, what's my next step?

G: Well, you can come in and we can meet.

J Okay.

G: And then, you know…see.

J: I know I met you, but….

G: Where did we meet?

J: We met at The Playboy Mansion.

G: I don't remember things like that.

J: I gave you my card; it was the only one in full color.

G: Yeah, when did you do that? Recently?

J: Yeah, at this last party at The Midsummer Night Dream.

G: Okay.

J: Blonde.

G: Where do you live?

J: Arizona.

G: Oh, we just talked.

J: Yeah.

G: Yesterday. Oh, of course.

J: Yeah. That's why I felt bad when you called me on the phone I was driving in the car….

G: Oh, I see. No…I mean, what I told you was to send me some more of those pictures.

J: Okay.

G: And, I will get them to Marilyn. She is the main person and then you can get a test.

J: Okay. Even like, special edition?

G: No, no....forget that right now.

J: Okay.

G: The special editions I can put in whoever I want.

J: Okay.

G: I mean, that's done. I mean, that's easy. All I have to do is call up and say, "I want this girl, this girl, this girl..." They do it. I mean, I've got serious clout here.

J: That's awesome.

G: And then, um...basically um, then what I'll do is I can get your pictures over to the —, which is Marilyn Gabowski and then she will tell me whether she wants to test you or not. If she does, then you'll go down there and you'll do a test and if they like you, then you're in.

J: Can...I kind of want to just do like Jordan did.

G: That's going to be tough, because you have to be famous already.

J: Right.

G: The only way to get a cover or a pictorial, you've got to be very well known. Jordan was very well known in London, so she was able to get a cover. A girl that is just a Playmate does not get a cover.

J: Yeah. Right, I just think that Hef has so many Playmates already picked out.

G: My point is that you don't get a cover if you're a Playmate.

J: Exactly.

G: You have to be able to sell magazines. Okay. I mean, if you've gotten a series or if you've gotten a TV show or a movie and you're on your way to stardom, then you might be able to get a cover. Or, just your name on the front and then a pictorial inside, which you can get money for. For instance, like Brooke Burk or someone like that. But, you're not going to get a cover just being ....without doing anything. There's no way. They've got to sell magazines and ...

J: Right. I don't care about the cover. I just meant....you know how they have those little articles inside there, further back ...

G: Right. They are not going to do that unless you've got some story to tell.

J: Right. Which I do. I'm a professional poker player. I've made the cover of all those magazines.

G: The only way that they care about that is if you are the world's champion.

J: Okay. Well, I appreciate that. See, this is what I need to know though.

G: Well. That's the truth.

J: That's why I'm so glad I met you.

G: I mean, I started out...I repped Pamela Anderson before she was Playmate. I mean, I've repped her. I made her deal for Baywatch. I was at William-Morris at the time. I got her into Baywatch. I got Donna Dericco. I met her in Vegas. I got her in *Playboy*. Um, I got her on Baywatch. Um, Tracy Bingham; Carmen Electra; Jenny McCarthy....I got Jenny McCarthy on Singled Out and then I got her in *Playboy*. I mean, you know...that's what I do. That's how I built up my relationship with *Playboy*. So, they pretty much let me...when there was a strike in the commercial business and they said, "Why don't you come with us? We'll make you a VP and then you can have your own agency too."

J: Wow.

G: So, I said "Okay," you know? So, basically, that's what I am. I'm VP of promotion and I also have my own agency. Yeah, well Marilyn...

J: I've met Marilyn before.

G: Marilyn is a bit odd. Marilyn is very ....she has her own way of doing things, but when I get ahold of her, she does what I tell her and um....and that's pretty much how it works. But, I knew Jordan from London, and I flew Jordan out here as her manager.

J: Yeah. She is a beautiful girl.

G: And, you know, she had done every cover. Like, last year, I did every cover of Stuff, every cover, and I did seven covers of Maxim and I did every cover of European Stuff and you know, I'm known for that. This is my gig. This is what I'm known for. I have the sexiest and best girls in the country.

J: Well, I'm so excited that you gave me your card. That's an honor.

G: Well.

J: Even if...

G: Yeah, but I mean...if you see the girls I have, you will know all of them and you'll say, "Wow," you know? So, you know, every famous girl from Frederick's, every famous pin-up girl, every girl that's got the top web sites, those all the girls I represent.

J: Okay...so, I just...

G: I handle every aspect of their career.

J: You do?

G: You open the magazine and you see, like, you know, Skyy Blue? Those ads? That girl is mine. And, when you see, like....commercials with sexy girls in beer commercials or commercials, like I have a Midas commercial where there are two girls in the Jacuzzi and … a Valvoline commercial. I just….all kinds of commercials where you see all these ads for um….for Cutty Shark and for all these different whiskeys where they have really sexy girls, like wrapped in nothing, those are all my girls.

J: That's so fun.

G: Yeah.

J: No wonder you're at the Playboy Mansion.

G: Well, it's a separate issue because I'm not employed, I mean…I'm a VP, but before I was an employee, I was friends with Hefner and… um… he always, you know, considered me like a junior version of him. So, I was always invited up there since I was sixteen.

J: Really?

G: Yeah. So, I've been going there for a long time.

J: That's so awesome.

G: Yeah. So, basically, you know I'm the only guy in this city that does what I do.

J: That's so cool.

G: Yeah. It's good. So, um….I can help you out.

J: Well, I'd sure appreciate any – you know….

G: Yeah. No problem, just, you know….send me some more shots, and I'll send them to Marilyn and I'll send them to Hef also and …

J: Yeah. I've sent them to Hef already. I lived at the mansion for a week.

G: Well, then you know him.

J: Yeah, but…

G: Well the whole thing is…. Let me tell you something. I don't believe in all that kind of stuff. It's a joke, okay? All those old men ogling at the young girls. I mean, the whole point of that….you know when a girl tests for *Playboy*, the biggest issue that I have with it is that you have to be on parade for all those old men. And, a lot of girls don't like that, going out every single night and…you know, I don't do that. When I submit a girl for *Playboy*, you know, they take me seriously. When a girl goes by herself or when like one of his cronies like, Sagenor or Ron Smith or one of those guys, then it's free game. Then it's not serious. Then, "Okay, we'll make you a Playmate, but we're not going to give you a month." Okay? And then if you don't do what we tell you to do, you're not going to be a Playmate.

J: Exactly. And, that's why I came home.

G: Right. Okay? So, but like when I do…

J: I didn't participate.

G: No, and I'll give you another story like, when Marilyn, she has her guys too and then, it's like, she promised me that she would make this girl a Playmate, promised me. Wrote me a letter; took me to lunch and took me to dinner because this Arab guy wanted her so badly and then he wouldn't go through with it because she was married and then…so, she got taken out. They wouldn't let her be a Playmate. Which is totally absurd and ridiculous? But, that's how politics are. You know something? Fuck it. You know, once you become famous and once you get a series, and once you get on a TV show and you're well known, them you can go back to them and ask for like $100,000 or $200,000 bucks, then you can be on the cover. Then you can do what Jordan did. Then you can be, like have five pages inside and do that kind of thing. That's the right way to do it.

J: Well, the sad thing with the Playmates is almost every one of his girl-friends have already, you know…

G: Well, they all left him. They are disgusted. The ones he has now are like missing teeth and they are like, gross. But, you know….

J: Yeah, but then he realized that they would leave him if they were too gorgeous.

G: Well, most of the ones have now. They all have. The ones you see now are ugly.

J: And they, I stayed with them. You know, I went partying with them for a couple of days when I was there and they still are promised different things.

G: Oh, I know. I mean, I had a girl that they called up. This is between us; there is a girl that shall be nameless called me up and said, "Hey, listen, I want you to meet this girl." Just to get her off his back or whatever, just to promise her something. And, I'm telling you, this girl was just like so ugly and so pathetic. She was so ugly. And then, so—not good.

J: That's why it was so sad when I went to the party; it was like, "Okay."

G: I said, "When are you going to be a Playmate?" And she says, "Well, I'm going to be one, but I don't have a month yet." And that automatically means you're not gonna be one. But that just means, you know… You know what it implicates.

J: I know exactly because I was there and …

G: Yeah. You know how it works.

J: And, I came home and it was like sad.

G: It gave you a bad taste in your mouth.

J: The only reason it was sad, too, is because I haven't done any modeling. I've only done a little bit and I feel bad. I'm like…

G: If someone wants to do the flats, fine. If someone wants to be a Playmate, fine. But, other than that I don't do any of Playboy's work. I don't do any nude work. I don't do any—nothing. I mean, all I do is big money commercials and where they want really sexy girls, that's it. When you see a sexy girl in a hot tub in a commercial or in a bar —that's me.

J: When I went to the ranch and even to the birthday party, I do like how many sit-ups a day and work out…

G: You look great. I saw you. I mean…

J: And I was even as good then as when you saw me.

G: I saw everything with your little angel wings on.

J: I was even in better shape before. I was already kind of like was fat and …

G: I wouldn't worry about it.

J: I mean I still was in fairly good shape, but…

G: Why didn't you test while you were here?

J: Um…

G: You didn't want to?

J: No, I don't think I had a choice.

G: What do you mean?

J: I don't know. I mean I wasn't asked or anything.

G: You just have to do it.

J: Yeah.

G: You just have to go… I mean, what I do is I just get good photographers to shoot girls and if they have good pictures, I just get them to Marilyn and I say, "Listen, leave this girl alone. She is under my control." And, then it's taken professionally. It's not… That's the difference. If you go up there and try to be a Playmate and you're stuck.

J: Right. I just can't do that.

G: No. Of course not.

J: So...

G: I don't blame you. So, you know that's the right way to be.

J: Well, I sure appreciate it. I e-mailed you a couple of pictures from a shoot I did last week.

G: I mean I'll help you out. No problem.

J: And I'll take care of you. Not sexually though. I can give you money.

G: I didn't expect that.

J: For all of your time or anything.

G: I don't do that. That's why I'm sitting in this office. I don't go out or date any of my models. Well, I can't say that. I have, a few, but...not many of them.

J: Some girls are ....you know, I mean, if it's not a trade thing, it's different.

G: Never that. It's a mutual thing.

J: If you like them it's different. It's just...

G: Exactly, it's a mutual thing, but it's a rarity.

J: Yeah.

G: So, let me know what you want to do.

J: Okay, I appreciate it so much.

G: I can put you in a flat in one second. You have probably done the flats already.

J: Did you ever go to my *Playboy* site?

G: No.

J: On that card I sent you, if you type that whole long gigantic address in, it shows all the pictures from that one day shoot.

G: The shot that you sent me looked like it was from the flats, it looked like a *Playboy* photographer shot it.

J: Right. It is.

G: So, you didn't do the flats?

J: I don't know what a flat is. I'm sorry.

G: Flats are the newsstand specials.

J: No.

G: Like, we have an issue out.

J: Is it an exclusive pictorial?

G: We have an issue out right now called Voluptuous Vixens, which is perfect for you.

J: Yeah. I would love to do any of that.

G: You can do it.

J: That would be awesome.

G: Well, if you send me some Xerox copies, I'll send some down to Marilyn and then Ill send some over to Kevin – not Kevin, but, Jeff Cohen in Chicago is the one that picks and he lets me put in any girl I want.

J: Okay.

G: So, send some of those to me. Let me know next time you're coming
out, and we will go from there.

J: Thank you so much. Have a great day.

Since he told me if I didn't get to L.A., he would come to Arizona and
pack me up himself, we decided to buy a motor home to fulfill my crazy dream.
The manufacturer told us it would be ready before Thanksgiving. Of course,
it wasn't, and I informed Gordon that I would be living in L.A. as soon as it
was ready. After numerous delays with the motor home I decided to fly with
my dog and announce to Gordon that I was living in L.A. I moved into a hotel
call the Sofitel about two miles from his office. This was December. I had a
terrible first day. Either I had the flu or food poisoning. I started feeling really
ill when I got off the plane, and by the time I checked into my room I was sick
the rest of the day and into the night. I walked across the street to get some
kind of medicine. I got the attention of the pharmacist and as soon as he
walked over to me I vomited all over the floor and they rushed me into the
bathroom so that I could finish. I called Bruce from the restroom lying on the
floor, feeling so low, lonely, embarrassed, and scared. Thank god for my dog,
because she got me through the night.

I felt better the next day, got a cab and headed to Gordon's office. I was
in full *Playboy* regalia. It was a true *Playboy* office with the logo, reception-
ist, security guard with the official *Playboy* pin. I waited in the lobby while
the woman announced that I was there surrounded by *Playboy* magazine and
a gigantic 3-D *Playboy* logo on the wall. Gordon escorted me to his office.
He started the conversation by asking me about my personal life. I asked him
if I looked the same, and he responded that I looked even better than he
remembered. I had some other photos that he hadn't seen and showed them
to him. They were on a disk. He selected one that he liked best and needed
twenty prints dropped off at his office the following day. He said they were
very good but felt they were a little too "*Playboy* looking." He wanted to
book me on a variety of venues, and these pictures portrayed me only as a
sexy blonde and he was going to need something more plain—he called it an
acting shot. He gave me the numbers of three photographers he felt were
excellent and showed me samples of their work. He felt the best of the three
was a guy named Bill. After he showed me the other photos I agreed that I
needed a more versatile portfolio and said I would call Bill.

I was very excited. I mean, this was L.A. Hollywood! He showed me many of the girls he was representing, and the walls were covered with photos, ads he had done, and many other projects he had been involved with. I started pointing out many of the girls that were current girlfriends of Hef. He represented more than half of his girlfriends.

Gordon gave me his contact numbers, told me to call him anytime and that we should get together for lunch or dinner since I didn't know the area. I spent hours at a local Kinko's shop getting the photo off a Mac disk, and then printed. I finally got to bed and had a courier drop the photos at his office the next day. I called him to make certain he had received them. The next day there was no call from Gordon. I assumed that with all his enthusiasm for me I would be running around to lots of auditions right away. I decided to call him at one o'clock and mention dinner as the reason for my call.

"Hi. It's Jill Ann. I just wanted to tell you that if you wanted to go to dinner tonight, I'm free."

"Good thing you called," he said. "What are you doing right now?"

"Nothing. Just waiting at the hotel in case you called to send me anywhere."

"I've got a spot if you can get there between 3:00 and 4:00. They're looking for *Playboy*-type girls. Can you come across as beautiful but mean and willing to pretend to be fighting in a bathing suit?"

Of course I could. He told me to wear a bathing suit under my clothes and get out there. He started naming off many of the gigs that he had placed girls: Levi ads, Cutty Shark, Miller Lite, Stuff, Maxim. The list went on and on. He told me that the girl on cover of *Playboy* a month or so ago, Jordan, was his placement. He contracted that deal, and he brought her to Playboy. He also told me that he brought Pamela Anderson and Carmen Electra in. To hear this was incredible. The dreamer in me believed every word and thought this guy was my ticket.

After I did my hair and makeup I grabbed a cab for Santa Monica. It was a Miller Lite commercial. I auditioned and was very nervous. They asked me to do a somersault, but I got dizzy and couldn't sit up for a few seconds. I think that was the nail in my coffin, but that was the first audition for a commercial I had ever done and I was pretty excited about it. There were a lot of girls there, and most of them were from Gordon Rael's agency. I spoke to another girl, not from Gordon's agency but had been many years ago, who told me she had already been on two commercial tests that morning. I figured I had better rent a car if I was going to do a lot of running around. I was reluctant because I didn't know my way around L.A., but seeing so many girls of Gordon's agency gave me great hope.

I called Gordon later that day to thank him for sending me on the audition. We set up lunch for Saturday.

He said, "I told you I was legitimate."

"Yes, you are. I'm so relieved. Thanks for saying so many nice things about me. I'd pretty much given up on the whole modeling thing after the *Playboy* mansion deal. Thanks for representing me."

"So are you going to move out here, then?"

I told him, "I've already moved. Don't worry about me staying at a hotel. Just consider me here and ready to work. I'll be parking the motor home in Malibu which is situated close to anywhere I need to go."

"Aren't you afraid to drive a motor home?"

"Oh, I won't be driving it. Bruce will."

He wanted to know who Bruce was and I told him he was my boyfriend, that he was moving with me and that I would be afraid to move to L.A. alone. He then said he had a million things to do and hung up.

I called up an acquaintence of mine who was living in Arizona but had moved to LA, "Kim" and told her I was in LA. We made a plan to get together and go out the next day. She wanted to see my pictures and hear about my adventures. Kim and I got together and visited for hours in my hotel room. She had gotten to meet Hugh Hefner at Glamourcon recently. She was going to the mansion the upcoming Saturday for a private event, and she was really excited. After seeing my pictures of me out with Hef and his girlfriends, she got enthused when she saw an ethnic girl among them. She thought he only liked blondes. The girl was Melissa. She told me she wanted to be a girlfriend and go out in the limo and do all the fun things. I felt I had to warn her about what really goes on because she needed to know. She didn't care. I told her they don't use protection. She didn't care about that either. She loved *Playboy* and everything about it. I suggested that she give him her number when she went Saturday. She said she already had at Glamourcon. I offered to go with her to the bar that Hef frequented and she could talk to him there. That got her attention and she wanted to include me in her evening plans, and we could hit Hef's bar afterward.

She was so excited and then said she was supposed to go on a date with this guy that night and wondered if she should cancel. She offered that I could come along as he had a brother who lived with him. I told her that I had a boyfriend. She assured me it wouldn't be a date. They had a million-dollar house right off Sunset Boulevard and a Ferrari, a Mercedes SUV, and a BMW!

She said the house was incredible and not to worry; we could just visit a while and get a free meal. She was starving and as soon as she ate we would leave to find Hef. I thought it would be fun, and I really did want to see the house and cars. She picked me up at the hotel, and we drove to the brothers' house. I was expecting the brothers to be Asian and dorky. They were dorky but white. I had my dog with me, and as I walked in I started laughing. They wanted to know what was funny, and I told them my misconception.

The house was beautiful with what seemed to be miles of white marble flooring but minimal furniture. I had taken my dog outside. A large pool was situated so that you could see passersby. One of the brothers came out and suddenly said as he looked at the street, "That's Tobey—Spider Man." He was passing by in his car.

Being star struck I was excited. He said that Britney Spears lived two streets up, and Leo DeCaprio lived on such and such a street and pointed towards the distance. He then told me he had his nails done at a place nearby and that Britney Spears had walked in. She observed he was getting "the works": one person giving him a pedicure, another giving him a manicure, and a third giving him a massage. I told him I wanted to know where the nail place was so I could go there. We finally headed out. They offered me some sort of drink. I told them I only drank Malibu and rum and asked if they had a Diet Coke. They said no so I took what they offered but didn't drink it. I got to ride in the Ferrari—the door opened straight up which was really neat. The dog's bag wouldn't fit so they put my dog and her bag in the Mercedes. Of course, Kim and I took pictures of us in front of the Ferrari. We went a short distance with him complaining about how the car only got eight miles to the gallon and he didn't drive it often. The ride was exciting. I had never been in one before.

We went through a back entrance to get into a very exclusive club. When we got to the security area, they recognized the boys and were excited to see them. They let us in right away. When we were seated we ordered one round of drinks and tried to order food, but the waitress told us it was too late for food. Kim did not look happy. I didn't really care because I didn't want to owe anyone for food. I even offered to pay for my drink when it came. The guy that I was with never came back to the table. He was gone pretty much the entire time. When I excused myself to go to the restroom I saw him with a girl up against the wall talking to her. When I came out she was handing him her phone number. I felt like I was a goldfish swimming with sharks! After a while he returned to the table and told me that the encounter was just business. They were in an internet business. It sounded like a pyramid scheme to me. I just smiled—I didn't really care. We didn't even get to order a second drink when they asked for the check. They let us know we were going back to their house.

This time my dog was in her travel case—luckily, or I would have been a nervous wreck. I didn't know Kim that well, and I didn't know where I was—what if they stole my dog? Holdem was my baby! I had been back at the guys' house about twenty minutes before Kim returned. She said something about getting lost. She told me she was going to go freshen up. She acted as though she was looking for my approval so I said okay. I and another couple there watched TV. An hour passed without a word between the one brother and me. Kim was still freshening up I guess, since she had not returned. The couple asked me a few general questions. They told me my "date" (not really, but the brother I was hanging out with) was completely afraid of little dogs, and they couldn't believe he was being so cool. He smiled and I apologized. I had no idea so I put her in her bag. He then left the room for what seemed a very long time.

I finally decided that it was time I left. I knocked on the door to tell the brother that I was going to call a cab and head home. I had to look fresh for my agent the next morning. He went to get me the number of a cab company, and I knocked on the bedroom door behind which Kim and her date had gone, to tell her I was leaving. She wanted to know how I was getting home. I told her I was taking a cab. She came out and talked the brother into taking me. We took the Mercedes SUV, and he pointed out where Britney Spears gets her nails done.

I wasn't happy with Kim. She pretty well ditched me as far as I was concerned. However, she did take the time to throw a fit that I was taking a cab and got the guy to drive me the two miles back to my hotel. Being a liberal girl I wasn't surprised how the whole night went. To top it off, Bruce was hopping mad about me going on a "double date." I knew I would never hear the end of it. I explained to him that before going with Kim I had told him all about what she had told me about the house, the cars, and he had said I could go, but I really shouldn't have gone. As it turned out the evening was a disaster. We never even made it to the bar that Hef frequented, which was Kim's big focus. She called me the following day and was still at the guys' house. She was getting ready to go to the *Playboy* mansion for the Private event.

Saturday I called Gordon to find out what time we were meeting for lunch. He told me that his plans had changed. He had a large job, and it was urgent. We decided to reschedule. I had planned to meet with the photographer on

Sunday, and we did the shoot. The guy was a little stressed out which ultimately led to a huge argument between him and the make-up artist. She
finally redid the makeup and was about to cuss out the photographer, but I put
my finger to my lips. "Don't go there." I didn't want the tension between the
two of them to influence how my pictures came out! Because the shoot took
twice as long as normal I had to change my return flight reservations. He shot
all the photos digitally and kept running to his computer to look at them. He
thought they were great. The makeup gal and I became friends, and we e-
mailed for awhile. She actually did my makeup for the New Year's Eve party
at the *Playboy* mansion.

I let Gordon know that I was going back to Arizona for a few days to get
more clothes. He said that he didn't want to send me out on any more auditions until we got the pictures back and printed from the photographer because he wanted them to be the best and the ones he had just weren't good
enough. I told him I would stay until the photographer got them back and we
could print them. He agreed and said that with the holidays no one was doing
much work. It would probably be after the first of the year. That worked for
me because I wanted to spend Christmas in Arizona. From our conversation,
I got the impression that he didn't care when or if I came back.

My associations with Gordon and the photographer went downhill over
the course of the next several weeks. Getting him the photos turned out to be
very difficult, and finally the photographer wouldn't return my calls. How
hard would it have been for the photographer to get the disk of my photos to
Gordon or me? I was really upset. I talked Bruce into heading to LA so that
I could get this completed. We drove to the photographer's real job at some
back alley place, got the disk and drove it to Gordon's office. Gordon didn't
like the pictures and gave me two more names to contact. I wasn't happy.
My career was on hold, and I was unable to do anything to further it. I was
really getting frustrated. I let him have it. If he didn't feel I had what it took,
then I wanted to know it and stop fooling around wasting my time. He reassured me telling me that I did have what it took—he just didn't realize I was
so serious about being a model or he wouldn't have suggested that particular
individual and gave me two other numbers. I apologized for overreacting and
told him that I had a lot of problems in California and that I wanted to get all of
my feelings out on the table. I got in touch with one of the photographers'
names he'd given me.

It was at least a studio even though he lived at the studio. The last photographer we shot it in his apartment with moving the kitchen table out of the
way. This photographer used film instead of digital. I had to pay for a

makeup artist/hairstylist, a stylist for my wardrobe, and the photographer, but it wasn't much more than the last shoot. The makeup artist started talking with me, and this whole experience with Gordon came out. She wondered about how I had decided to use this particular photographer. I told her Gordon Rael had recommended him after the first one didn't do them well enough. She filled me in on some other agents and how they operated.

I asked her if she knew anything about Gordon. She told me he was just as bad and that she had heard it from a variety of girls. The rumor in L.A. was that Gordon apparently got kickbacks from photographers that he recommends. I was furious. My hands shook, and I know my face got very red. I felt used and lied to.

She continued to give me advice about the modeling world in L.A. She told me to never, ever go anywhere without Bruce. There were lots of agencies, and if he came with me they would know it was strictly for business. The photos came out very well and about a week later I needed to contact Gordon because he was the one, he told me, who decided which ones would go on my Zed card. That is a group of photos showing different looks and styles to highlight your modeling range. I headed into Gordon Rael's office and left Bruce in the car with the dog. The secretary announced me and after about half an hour she called him to remind him I was still waiting. He appeared after about another forty-five minutes.

He was talking about ninety miles an hour and could hardly stand. At one point he asked my opinion of a particular photo. I told him he was the professional, and I would go with whatever he selected. As he moved over to have me look at the picture he nearly fell over, and I wound up holding onto him until he got back upright. While I was there many phone calls were patched through—some he took, some he didn't. He stumbled from the photo display area to his desk and back. He started talking about many of his favorite things: caviar, very expensive wines, and many delicacies of which I had never heard.

I thanked him and left to get the photos he picked made into four by sixes. Once they were printed I took them to a place called Bunker that Gordon had referred me to for the Zed card. At the shop where I stopped to have the 8 x 10 headshot done, I found dozens of pictures of Playmates and current girlfriends. Bruce suggested I have one printed like theirs. I ordered one hundred of them. It was a picture that *Playboy* had taken of me for the shoot that was fully clothed with me holding cards. We had downloaded the picture from the internet. It read: "Jill Ann Spaulding 2002 Playboy's Queen of Hearts." On the *Playboy* site it said at the top of my pictorial Queen of

Hearts so this is where I had gotten this from. They put the little Playboy logo and listed Gordon's phone number for booking information on the picture. The same day they were printed, I went up and down Melrose Street autographing them and gave them to many stores that had pictures posted. I was just having fun, being spontaneous. I was so happy. I felt like a princess. I still had not been called to any interviews or casting calls and nothing from Gordon.

Kim, whom I had forgiven, Bruce, and I went shopping on Melrose quite a few times, and she never gave up on her insistence to meet Hef. I relented, and we booked a table for three at his favorite spot, a very hot A-list club. We arrived before Hef and his usual bevy of beauties did. Kim had left her car at our hotel, and Bruce and I drove her in ours. After we ordered our meal, I saw Hef arrive.

"Okay, there he is. Head on back."

She couldn't get up the nerve and came back begging me to go with her. I agreed. We headed into the ladies room for a moment. Coming back out, I spoke to one of the bodyguards.

I said, "I called and spoke to Marilyn Grabowsi, telling her that I was going to bring a friend to introduce to Hef." This was the truth, I did call and spoke to Marilyn and asked them which club Hef was going to be at that night and told her I wanted to introduce Hef to one of my girlfriends.

"I wasn't informed," he said. "It would be better if you come back when he's on the dance floor. He'll come over and talk much easier if he's already up."

I thanked him, and we headed back to our table. About ten minutes later, we tried again. Bruce had told me that if I got in to just stay and enjoy myself. Many of the girlfriends came over to me and gave me hugs saying they were excited to see me. In reality, they were blocking Hef's ability to see who wanted to get his attention. I figured this out right away. They wondered what I wanted. I told them my friend was in love with *Playboy* and just was afraid to come to Hef and introduce herself. They could tell we weren't leaving and made their way back to the dance floor.

Hef came over and acted pleased to see me and held Kim's hand. She had an intense letter in her hand that said she wanted to be a Playmate and make love with him. He didn't look at it, but slipped it into his front pocket. He wrote Kim's number on a pad of paper that already had another girl's name above it. Maybe he was collecting numbers. She asked him if we could come in, and he shook his head no. Then he went back to dancing with his girlfriends without another word.

Kim turned to me looking so disappointed. "Do something."

"Are you sure you want me to?" I asked. She nodded.

I tapped the bodyguard on the shoulder. Pointing to Kim I said, "She wants to have sex with him. Can you tell him that?" He smiled and walked over to Hef. Kim was standing slightly behind me.

Hef came over to me and asked, "What do you need?"

"She wants to have sex with you."

Without a word he lifted the rope and in we went. We started dancing. The girls realized we had broken the barrier and asked us if we wanted something to drink. We ordered. The club lights were pulsating, and as usual, the girls were dressed in clothing that made them the stars of the club.

We weren't there long when Hef spoke to Kim. "You can come home with us, but your friend can't."

She told me what he said, and I felt very uncomfortable being there.

She asked, "Why does he have something against you?"

"I didn't sleep with him." She gave me a sad look, hugged me and thanked me for getting her into the circle.

"You got yourself in."

I didn't stay that long. Bruce had already come over and taken pictures of Kim and me dancing. There were no happy vibes coming from the girls. One girl, just like Kelly, had attached herself to Kim telling her she would take care of her. Kim didn't seem to be so afraid anymore and didn't seem to need me. I sneaked out and went back to the table with Bruce. We ate in silence for a while.

Bruce said, "You should have stayed."

I shook my head. "No. They really didn't want me there."

I did decide to go back and bring my dog to show the girls. The bodyguards were upset because I had gotten through the side, and they didn't see the dog. They looked pretty upset that I had gotten in without their knowledge. They were all getting ready to leave. Kim hugged me, and I went back to Bruce. We watched as the group left the club and into the limo I knew was waiting. Kim waved on the way out.

The following day at about ten in the morning we heard a knock on the door of our hotel room at the Sofitel. It was Kim. She came into the room and started telling us what had gone on. She said they all took turns giving him a blow job and while Hef was having sex with one of the girls, Deborah was shoving her finger up his ass. I offered an "I told you so," but she said that until she had seen it for herself she couldn't have believed it. She had not slept with him, but she watched. She told me that she ended up staying in Destiny's room afterwards, and they ordered room service and talked all night. She explained having to wear the pink pajamas, having to take the bath prior and Hef taking a picture of her in the bathtub. Kim told us she hadn't slept the entire night and needed to eat. She was exhausted but said that she had the best time and she really wanted to be a girlfriend. We walked down to the valet so she could get her car and took her out for dinner so we could hear more gossip.

The following week Hef himself called Kim asking her to go out with him and his girlfriends and to be at the mansion at 10:00 p.m. She was so excited. I couldn't believe Hef had called her himself and thought that pretty cool. Kim called me the next day to tell me all about it. She had arrived at the mansion a little ahead of schedule, dressed and ready to go. The same things happened that night, except at the very first bar one of the girlfriends had ordered shots and Kim drank a lot of them. She became so sick that the bodyguards had to take her back to the mansion. She threw up in the car on the way. The rest of the group went on without her and returned to the mansion later in the evening. She thought she had alcohol poisoning. I asked her if she had slept with him and she told me she hadn't because she couldn't even hold her head up. I wondered if she had gone up to watch and she said no. She was upset. She felt that she had completely ruined her chances of being a girlfriend after what had happened. I told her she was crazy. Hef wouldn't be mad at her; she hadn't messed up her chances. She was nearly hysterical. I talked to her a long time to try to calm her down. I told her that the same gal had tried to get me to drink shots when I was there. I just took them and sipped them, like I was drinking them and then discarded them so that the waitress would pick up the glass so I wouldn't get sick. I told her that I didn't trust the girls and that maybe they would purposely put something in her drink. She was so sick she didn't leave her house for days. I kept calling to check on her but she didn't want to go out or do anything she felt so ill. When she explained me the array that she had to drink I told her to never mix alcohol. If she planned on drinking she should stick with the same drink all night.

Hef finally contacted her and invited her to go out with him and his girl-friends and told her not to drink so much. She was elated to get a second chance. I told her that since she hadn't slept with him, he wasn't going to give up that easily. She met up with the group at the appointed hour, and they all did the photo prior to going out. The same thing happened this night that had happened all the other nights, but this time Kim finally did sleep with him. She stayed up most of the night talking to Julie and a few of the other girls. Julie was a new official girlfriend that was not there at the time I was Upstairs. She felt that since she had finally slept with him that she and the girls shared an instant bond and seemed to feel a little more at ease with them after this. Destiny told her that the group had preset plans and that they would contact her the following week.

* * * * *

January 19, 2003: *I had heard that the Golden Globes were at the Beverly Hills Hotel so I asked Bruce to head down there with me so I could somehow get in. It was a spur of the moment thing, and Bruce dropped me off and I told him I would meet him down the street by the Starbucks when I was done. I walked up and tried to pretend I was on the In-Style List. They didn't fall for it. There were many different lines and different parties and different lists. I stood there feeling a little stupid as movie stars started leaving from this same entrance. I moved to the side to watch the excitement. I wasn't there ten minutes until I saw Hef and his entire group of girlfriends coming out. The girlfriends saw me and didn't acknowledge me. I decided to say hello to Destiny who was in the back of the line. Hef came out holding Deborah's hand; everyone was accompanied by bodyguards and hopped into the huge SUV limo. Destiny said hi to me and quickly entered the limo. I was excited. I figured that the more they saw me at important events that it would promote me in their view. I walked back to where Bruce was parked, and we returned to the hotel. I called Kim and told her the not good news that Sherrie was there with Hef. Sherrie was a blonde who was not a girlfriend yet but had starting seeing Hef about the same time Kim had. Sherrie's first time sleeping with Hef was supposedly the same night Kim did, but she was there and Kim wasn't. Kim wasn't happy about that. I told her it must be just the blonde thing. We discussed the advisability of dying her hair blonde. She was upset and didn't understand why she was not invited. I decided to research Sherrie. I went to her personal website and on her bio page. It had this written, "One particular goal I am currently working on is becoming a Playboy Playmate that is my ultimate dream come true!!" The worst thing is when I went to the site it just brought back all of my memories of what I had gone through, but Kim had decided to take the next step. She had not walked down those stairs, out of that mansion. She was there trying to fulfill her dream.*

Kim decided to call up the mansion and asked to speak to Deborah. She was trying to win Deborah over and try to have her on her best side. She was asking her advice on anything she suggested she should do to fit in.

Deborah flat out said to her "You know, I don't appreciate sharing my boyfriend with other women, and I am not going to give you pointers." Then she hung up

January 23, 2003: *That weekend, having a connection with Jennifer Lewandowski in Chicago, I had an invitation for the San Diego Super Bowl party for Playboy for one female. Of course "female" did not mean Bruce Gifford my boyfriend. Once I got my invitation, I decided to order tickets for Bruce online for $1,000 and used my 25 percent Playboy model discount. We ended up in San Diego for the big Playboy party. Kim had not gotten an invitation so she was pretty upset. I told her it was probably because it was such short notice and that he had already purchased a certain number of seats. Just to get into the party was a staggering hour or more wait. I bluffed my way in using my Playboy card, and me, Bruce, and two other gals that I had hung out at the Playboy Mansion parties all got in without waiting.*

One person I noticed in the Hef group at the party was again Sherrie. I got to meet Tara Reid for the first time and get a picture with her. I also met Carmen Electra and Tom Arnold and got photos with both of them. Because I had my Playboy Jill Ann business card I was able to bluff my way to getting into the Playboy VIP section, and this was where all the stars hung out. Queen Latifah was there and said she doesn't allow photos taken after midnight because by then she has been partying for a while and doesn't like to have her picture taken. She was very nice, and she has a terrific smile. She invited us to sit with her and her group for a while. My poodle, Holdem, ran up to sit on her lap, and she seemed to love it. Carmen and Tara all took pictures with the dog and me. I couldn't get Bruce into the VIP room, much less into the party, but I had thought of a way around the problem. To get in, party-goers had to wear an illuminating 50 Playboy necklace. There was an outside terrace to the VIP area. I told Bruce my plan to have him wait on the other side and I would drop him the necklace—it worked perfectly (just a little ingenuity!). The party was very crowded, and if you weren't in the VIP room you were not having that great a time. With a ratio of 1 girl to 100 guys, talk about testosterone! For any guy who had paid $1,000 to get in there, basically there wasn't anyone to meet or look at. I felt badly about everyone who had paid so much to get into the regular party. In the VIP party, there were about ten Playmates and they were very nice to me since they were used to seeing my face at every event. We bid on a charity auction for two tickets to a Playboy party in New Orleans for two for $1005 and won. Bruce was included! I never spoke to any of the girlfriends or Hef that night. I just made sure that they had seen me.

* * * * *

Hef personally called Kim again asking her to go out with him and his girlfriends. She was very excited and felt everything was going her way. The major problem was that because she had to call off her shifts at Victoria's Secret to go to the mansion she no longer had a job. Her website had been completely set aside and the bi-monthly camera events she was supposed to do she hadn't done in months. Her personal updates had been neglected, and her webmaster was very upset. She was now three months behind on her rent and more than that on her car payments. The vision of being able to move into the mansion rent-free and have Hef buy her a car was an obsession. Some of the girls had confided in her that they got around a $2,000/week allowance and this made her even more motivated than ever. Do the math—$104,000 a year . . . and don't forget all the perks of free hairstyling, plastic surgery and clothing. Kim and I discussed her aspirations of being a girlfriend so many times because it did seem to be the answer to all her problems and that she would ultimately be in *Playboy*. It was the best of all worlds. The problem was that the landlord had already given her many opportunities to pay and it was only his crush that kept her from being tossed out on the street. She figured her car could be repossessed at any time and she would not be able to get anywhere without a car. She decided that she needed to write a letter to Hef. She had not had any time alone with him and the girls watched her all the time, so she figured if she wrote him a letter and told him to read it in private that then the girls wouldn't know exactly what was in it.

We met at the mall across from my hotel, and she bought a special Hello Kitty photo album, paper, and envelopes. We sat up most of the night writing the letter. I told her to try to make it as short and to the point as possible because he is so busy and that way he could read it without the girlfriends reading over his shoulder. Kim made notes. She made several drafts. By the end of the night this is what evolved:

Dear Hef:

I'm about to get evicted from my apartment. I'm three months behind in my rent. I lost my job from calling in sick every Wednesday and Friday. I can't concentrate on anything but being with you. I can't get enough of you. I've never done anal before but it looks fun, so I want you to be my first. If you could move me in 'til I get back on my feet I wanna lose my anal virginity to you, daddy! I will spend every hour of the day thinking of ways to please you.

Why did she write this letter? She was desperate. The anal part was just a tease hoping that would be enough to move her in. The girls that would let Hef have anal with them were his favorites, and I told Kim what Kelly had told me about Amber doing anal and that was why she got to live there so long. Also, during the sex orgy the only girl that gave Hef anal was Deborah, and this was why she was the number-one girlfriend. We called it "the anal edge." The next time Kim went to the mansion she gave the note to Hef and asked him to read it in private. The result of the note was that she was given $1,000 in cash.

The way this allowance system works I was told is he brings in each girl into his office one at a time because Saturdays are allowance days, and yes, girls do get different amounts and that is why they go in separately. Each is also sworn to silence on the amount or Hef would be upset. Girls will be girls, and they all talked. After sleeping with him that Friday night Kim was there until the handout of cash on Saturday. She even got her own private turn like the other girls. She explained to me that all of the girls were calling "Daddy, daddy, I need my allowance down the halls," and each one went and searched him out to get it. He did not ask her to move in, but he did give her some cash to get her by and she promised to pay him back when she could so that she did not seem demanding and said she would set up payments and make sure to repay him. He told her it was a gift, and he didn't want it back.

What did she do with the $1,000—pay bills? Yes, but some had to go for clothes for the upcoming Mardi Gras party at the mansion. She bought a $300 Coach purse when I was not with her, an entire outfit and a huge hat for the upcoming Mardi Gras party at the mansion. I told her not to, but she didn't listen. She felt that if she walked the part, looked the part, she would make girlfriend. She wanted to make the best impression ever, and when she went out on the town with Hef she wanted to have the best-looking outfits so that she would fit in. I ended up buying a diamond bra, even though I had already picked an outfit for Mardi Gras. The party coming up was the day after Valentine's Day, February 15th on Saturday.

That Friday Kim headed up to the mansion. It was Valentine's Day. All the girls had gotten gift baskets from Hef except for Kim—even including the new girl Sherrie. It was upsetting for Kim but she did not say anything. She spent the night Friday and woke up at the mansion Saturday in plenty of time to get ready for the big event that night.

Kim was told that they were not going out that Friday night because of the big party, but she didn't want to have to take the shuttle like all of the common folk since, after all, she was sleeping with the owner of the magazine and host of the party. She asked if she could come up the night before so that she would be on the premises before the party got started and she could get ready at the mansion. Hef agreed. I was sad because I didn't have her to ride up with to the party. We had already discussed that no matter what, that even during the party that she would not pay any attention to me . . . that she needed to stay at the table and play her girlfriend part. I told her not to get into trouble for talking to me and not to ask me to sit at the table with them. She deserved to be there, and so did the other girls. I would be fine.

The worst possible scenario happened to her. She and another girl had the identical outfits in different colors for the party. The other girl went running to Hef crying about it. Kim was asked not to wear hers, the outfit we had spent hours on selecting, and was loaned one from the girl who had complained. I didn't know about the incident until I saw Kim at the party and she overheard some of the girls saying that the other girl looked better in the ensemble than Kim.

The politics and backstabbing were incredible. I had prepared, as always, for the big party by driving miles to have my hair and makeup done, dressed at my makeup friend's house and Bruce drove me to the UCLA parking lot for the pickup. I kissed Bruce goodbye, and he waited at a distance to make sure I got on the bus without a hitch. There are lines and each person waits in the line that corresponds with the last name to make sure each is on the list. They check everyone's driver's license and place a band on everyone's arm. Then everyone goes to a different line where they take a current picture to make sure no one has gained weight or is looking ugly to decide who will be on the next party list. They call it "casting." Hef looks through the pictures and casts who he wants to be at his party and whom he doesn't.

On the bus ride, Pauly Shore was sitting in the seat behind me. He kept reaching through the chair dividers to get my attention. I just looked back at him, very flattered. The girls were all dressed very sexily and fully made up with glitter from head to toe, looking their best for the party. Everyone was playing with Mardi Gras beads and just being lively. When I got off the bus I headed to the very back of the mansion just to check out all the decorations and to pass by the exclusive Hef table to see what the girls were wearing.

I realized not having a girlfriend hanging around me was a sudden star magnet. I think this party, of all parties, I talked to more stars and they talked to me more than ever. I looked over and saw Ron Smith was talking to Michael Duncan Clarke from movies like "Green Mile" and "Dare Devil" standing at a little table all by himself. I, knowing Ron Smith, decided that this was a perfect opportunity for me to get to talk to Mr. Clarke. Who was Ron

Smith, one of Hef's Cronies as Gordon Rael described and he seemed to be at every Playboy Event and was at all the clubs that Hef frequented seated in a section near us.

I said "Hi Ron."

He said, "Hi, Jill Ann." I smiled. Ron turned back to talk to Michael Clarke and he was asking him to come up to the mansion the following day.

Michael looked over at me and said, "Is she going to be there?"

I smiled and Ron told Michael that he could bring me. Ron was then off to talk to others again.

I started to talk to Michael. I must admit Hef telling me I was no longer welcome to come up on Sundays because it was just too intimate of a day at the mansion made me want to go all the more. What am I talking about? When I moved to LA and told Gordon Rael that I was living in L.A. for good, I phoned the mansion and spoke to Jenny. I said, "I am living in L.A. now and was wondering if I could start coming up on Sundays for Fun in the Sun Day."

She said that she would talk to Hef and let me know. She called back later that day and said Hef said, "No, this is too intimate of a day for you to come up." My girlfriend Karen was up and had written a letter the week before telling Hef she was going to be in town and was wondering if she could come up for Fun in the Sun. He approved it. I said to Jenny you are letting my girlfriend Karen come up to this intimate day and approved her. Karen did go up that Sunday for Fun in the Sun. I, however, was not allowed to come.

I could not come up on Sundays and this was an opportunity to belie his intimation that I was not welcome. I couldn't be stopped if a star invited me—and this was intoxicating. My mind was whirling. I am such a bad girl. I could not help but really want this. I wanted all the girls to see me watching the movies with them, etc. Kim was going to be there also, and I could wave to her.

I barely talked to him but 10 minutes, I gave him my number, told him I would meet him at the mansion the following day and that was it. During the night I would see him in the distance and he would wink and I would wink and we never spoke again. The hook was set.

Late into the night I walked by the Hef table and Kim motioned me over.

She said, "Sit down."

I was scared. "No!"

She said, "No really, it's okay. I am bored out of my mind, and the other girls have had many of their friends sit down. It is okay."

Of course while we were sitting there, the cameras were on the Hef table the entire time filming every move. Kim started to adjust my diamond bra because it was slightly off-center and it snapped apart, busting open and revealing everything. Of course, the cameras were there to capture the entire moment and zoom in close.

I said, "You did that on purpose."

She helped me get it back together and then suddenly all of the girlfriends got up and hea*ded out*. She hugged me goodbye and headed upstairs with Hef and the girls.

Nothing else happened this night. Bruce picked me up. I went to sleep, and the following day I told Bruce that I was going to go to the Playboy mansion. I told him the whole thing about the Duncan guy and how excited I was just to see the girlfriends' faces when I showed up at the mansion for their Sunday event. He decided to head out and play a tournament at Ocean's Eleven which was about a 1½ hours away. I told him I would just take a cab to the Mansion. I called Kim on her cell phone at the mansion and she went outside to talk to me. I said that I noticed Michelle and one of the other girls come back down later on in the evening.

She said, "Yeah. You're not supposed to go back down. You can tell those girls don't really care if they get in trouble or not, but I did not go back down because I am not in yet and I am not going to make any mistakes."

I told her that I was planning on seeing her that night and she was so excited. I told her about the cab etc. I started to worry about the guards not letting me in. I decided to call the guards at the mansion and tell them the situation to make sure they were going to let me in. I said Ron Smith knows all about it. They said that Ron had not mentioned it to them and that he had not put me on the list. They gave me Ron's number so I called him.

He said, "Oh, that was something for you to work out between yourselves. That has nothing to do with me."

I told him I was going to be there and if I wasn't there Michael Clarke Duncan was probably not going to be happy. He said that as soon as he arrived he would call me and let me know if he wanted me there or not. I was so upset. I sat home for many hours until Bruce returned because I decided not to go. I was not going to beg at the gate and look like a fool or feel unwelcome. Bruce came back from the tournament and I was so glad to see him. I was so sad that my plan had not worked. We were sitting there watching TV, and my phone showed a message on my voice mail.

I really had no underhanded pretensions toward Bruce. I never tried to hide anything from him. Amazingly, Mr. Duncan called and left a voicemail. The message said: "Surprise! You didn't think I'd call you. I called and wanted to hear from you. Call me." He left me his number. I actually called back my voice message machine to have Bruce be able to hear the cool accent and message exactly. I was so excited. I told Bruce my whole intentions, and he seemed to understand my madness. I asked if I could go down into the lobby and call him back. Bruce wondered why I needed to go down to the lobby to call him back. I told him I wouldn't feel comfortable talking in front of him.

Bruce went absolutely ballistic. "You want to go and fucking flirt with a fucking man?"

I said, "No."

He said, "What the hell. Then you can make the fucking call from here. I'll just fucking go back to Arizona and you can fucking talk to him all you want."

I knew this was like the breaking point of our relationship that he was so pissed off and jealous and that I was in such deep water. I had been with this man for eleven years, but it had finally gotten to him. I had never pushed it this far, and I thought that at this moment I was losing the love of my life. He suddenly did not trust me anymore, and even though I felt so in control maybe he was right.

I picked up the phone with Bruce sitting on the bed to call Mr. Duncan. I said "Hi, it's Jill Ann."

He said, "I know who you are."

He asked if I went to the Playboy Mansion. I told him they wouldn't let me go unless I came with him. He said that he had so much to do he couldn't get away. I wished I could have explained my situation to him in person, or else in private, but I knew I had to discuss it in front of Bruce or we would be through.

Michael said, "What are you doing right now?"

I looked over at Bruce sitting staring at me.

"Not much."

He said, "Come over and see me."

"Oh, I can't tonight."

He said, "How about tomorrow night then?"

I told him that I was sorry that I misled him when I was at the Playboy Mansion. I was not myself. "I have a boyfriend," I finally said.

Michael now realized that even though we got along, and there had been some innocent flirting on my part, I would not let it go any further, and he was angry. "What! You fucking played me! You have a fucking boyfriend. You fucking played me! I don't want some used bitch that has a fucking boyfriend. Don't ever fucking call me again."

And then he hung up. Bruce looked at me and asked what he said.

I told him: "To never fucking call him again."

Bruce then was pissed off. "Who the hell does he think he is talking to you like that?"

I was so shocked. I heard the angriest person in my life on the other line of the phone. I was nearly shaking when I hung up the phone. What a night! I did not sleep well.

After the Mardi Gras party, Kim stayed that Saturday night. That night after the Mardi Gras party, Hef took the girls upstairs and the same orgy happened. He gives them Friday nights off if there is a party on Saturday night. Friday night they did not have the orgy; it was automatically moved to Saturday night. Kim said that Hef was kissing and hugging on her and acting like no one else was in the room. She stayed an additional night that Sunday night. The following morning she was in one of the girlfriends' rooms.

Hef came in and said to her, bluntly, "Kim you need to go, it's time for you to go." She didn't know what to say. She didn't say anything at all and just went to get her stuff and headed home. That was the last time that she would ever see Hef in person.

She called to speak to him later that week. He responded to her by saying, "Well, when we do go out I'll let you know." She hung up the phone after speaking to him.

Chapter Eight

I wanted to relate a few of the highlights of meeting movie stars at the Playboy Mansion. My impression was that it was like a private party, not a paparazzi event where everyone had to give interviews and pose for thousands upon thousands of pictures. It was a group of individuals who were all getting to party together—and that added to the atmosphere. There is a "vibe" there that most people will never get to experience.

The birthday party was my very first party and I remember seeing Keifer Sutherland, one of my absolute favorite actors, talking to a seemingly large group of people. Since I was alone and unaccompanied at the moment, I decided to tap on his shoulder just to say I loved his work. He never did turn around and the tapping did get a little more insistent. He and his group walked away and I, blonde, thought maybe if he notices that I'm a girl and not a guy he will at least acknowledge me. When he moved into an angle to see me with my pearly whites open wide he turned around with a snarl and gave me a foul look. The cameraman who had been nice to me earlier said to me, "Don't feel bad. He's a jerk to everyone." So, I have to say that sometimes getting to meet the people you idolize doesn't turn out the way you expect.

Weird Al was as goofy as always and very friendly.

I asked permission from Scott Baio's Playmate girlfriend to speak to him. Both of them were very understanding. No sneer from his beautiful lady, and she actually let him say a few words to me as he held my hand. I felt they were definitely a strong couple and really down to earth. Jon Lovitz smiled when I waved. Snoop Dog and his entire crew were passing by, and he gave me the "Hey baby!" as we passed each other.

I saw Melissa Rivers. I shouted, "Melissa! You look so cute!" She was wearing teddy bear PJ's that were not very revealing. I asked, "Do you approve?" (I spun around like they do on E!) She said, "With what you got you can get away with it."

Matthew Perry and David Schwimmer from *Friends* I met briefly and they all gave me a smile and seemed very friendly. Most of all the stars seemed to have a guest that they had brought with them to talk to, and they oftentimes they came with more than a few friends. This made it hard to talk to them because they just hung to themselves and really did not mingle. I took the initiative with all the celebrities to get their attention, and I was about the only one seeming to do it. Girls would follow me because they knew I would get the conversation started. I had heard from many people at the birthday party that the Midsummer Night's Dream party was the wildest party of them all. That this was the really wild one. When I arrived at this party I actually was really scared. I really was! There really was nothing but scantily clad girls walking around, but not too many other strange things such as people having sex.

One partygoer told me that when it gets late it starts getting crazy. I pictured a massive orgy or something—everyone having sex with everyone— but I thought to myself if this starts to happen I am going to leave the party early because I would not be not participating. However, nothing wild happened, no one even making out—and I stayed 'til almost the last bus back to the UCLA. More excitement was happening at a local bar than at this party. I talked to some of the girls at the party about how calm it was, and they said that there were so many producers, movie stars, etc. that you could not act out of character because you might lose your chance to be in a movie at a later point. I did not know what to believe. It was like a regular party with all the girls together in little groups, all the guys together in groups or two guys standing looking bored, and all the couples together. Many of the stars never got up from their tables the entire night.

Another party that I went to at the Playboy mansion was the Halloween party. This was actually one of the only parties that I actually drank more than I should have. I did feel slightly fat in my UPS outfit wearing next to nothing, and from dieting I had eaten hardly anything so the first drink I had hit me right away. The haunted house was really the best I had ever been through. At the Halloween party Karen and I hung out together most of the night. She laughed through the entire haunted house and was tickling many of the ghosts that tried to scare us. I was screaming, she was laughing.

We ran into Kelsey Grammar, and he was wearing a priest costume. He was very nice and let Karen and I pose next to him. We saw the late-night show host Craig Kilborn sitting all by himself by the pool.

Karen and I asked "Is there anyway we can get a picture with you?"

He said "I'm sorry, I don't do the picture thing, but I'll autograph something for you." We were very excited and I ran to get two napkins for him to sign. He began to sign both of them for us and then he said, "What the heck, I will let you take a picture."

I handed Karen my camera and went behind the table to pose with him. While I was smiling for the picture, he reached his hand up my UPS outfit and touched my genitals. I was posing, smiling, trying not to blink and he did this to me.

It was Karen's turn and as we switched the camera I told her, "Don't stand too close."

I motioned with my eyes really wide to warn her. I snapped the picture as quick as I could and reached back at the table to get the autographed napkins.

He said, "Why are you running off?"

"I'm Hef's girlfriend. He doesn't like me to be gone long."

We both hurried off. This is when Karen wondered what was that all about (the Hef girlfriend thing) I said he goosed me while you were taking the picture. She said he'd done the same to her. I just said the Hef's girlfriend thing hoping that he would be embarrassed and that he would be worried I would tell Hef what he had done.   My last star to meet, which was my first autographed *Playboy* that had started this whole thing, was Drew Barrymore. My girlfriends knew that I had missed her each and every party so they were not going to have me miss her again.

Karen said, "There's Drew."

"Where?"

She pointed her out. I started following and trying to get her attention. I started to speak and Drew turned completely around and started talking to her large group of friends she had brought with her to the party. I tapped her on the shoulders again and then they all decided to walk off. I had had a few Malibu's and Diet Coke so wasn't as shy as I normally was. One of the guys in the group happened to fall behind as they headed out and I let him have an earful.

I said "Do you know how much it would mean to me to have Drew talk to me? Do you have any idea that taking the minute to talk to me would mean so much   That she purposely turned away like that was so harsh."

I walked away. Later that evening, I saw Drew again outside with just a few of her friends about to light up a cigarette using Hugh Hefner's personal match book. I figured I had nothing to lose.

Karen was with me and I said, "Please Drew, is there any way I can get a picture with you?"

She said "Sure," and posed for the picture. I went on and on telling her how great she was and how much I loved her and told her I was sorry for acting so excited.

She said, "You're fine."

Karen was next, and both of us got a picture. When we got the pictures back, on different cameras, both were ruined. Huge lines went through the picture. We could not figure out how both cameras had done this. She was so upset with me that I had put my thumb in the picture and then when I got mine back it was even worse. I could barely make out the two of us. I always wondered if it was what I said that let her take a picture with her or if she was just a little nicer after the party got later. Who knows but I got to talk to her, and I still love her and think she is awesome!

* * * *

This trip, Bruce and I were at the hotel for fifty-two days. The photo shoot, getting pictures developed, and getting those pictures made into Zed cards all took time. I checked out of the hotel and dropped off everything at Gordon's office (the Zed cards, 8 by 10 head shots and the 8 by 10 *Playboy* pictures). My motor home was ready, so we drove to pick it up in Chino, California. We parked it in Malibu to live so that when Gordon called I would be within a half-hour drive to his office and near all surrounding areas. The following day I got a call from Gordon. I was excited to hear his voice.

He said, "Who gave you permission to use that picture of you with the cards."

I didn't know what to say. "Hef did."

"Okay." He hung up. That was it.

A few weeks went by, and Kim still felt bewildered and still wanted to live at the mansion or be part of *Playboy*. She visited me in Arizona, and I tried to be supportive. I told her she would have to gather her courage and call Hef again. I was in the room with her when she called. She was very upset as she worked herself up into making the call, and said, "What the hell does he mean 'when we go out'? That means he's not going to fucking call me because they go out every Wednesday and Friday night." She was so upset.

Then I got a phone call from a man at *Playboy*. He told me he had spoken with Hef, and he had not given me permission; that even if he had, he didn't have the right to give me permission. He told me that I must stop using the pictures and that they must be returned to their office immediately. I was told I would be receiving a letter from Chicago that I needed to sign and return agreeing not to use the *Playboy* logo or picture. He was very cold and very firm. I asked for the address and returned them as soon as possible. I asked if I had to return my business cards that had the logo on them as well. He told me all of it had to be returned or I was open to a lawsuit.

I hung up the phone and started crying. Kim and Bruce were there. I decided to call the Playboy Mansion. I was transferred to Hef's personal secretary. I told her what had happened. She told me that if I cooperated everything would be fine. I was crying uncontrollably worrying that Hef was angry with me. She assured me he wasn't. I mailed the photos and my business cards to Gordon's office.

After two weeks I still hadn't received a letter from Chicago. I called and spoke to the same man who had called me, gave him my grandparents' address and mentioned I had not received the letter he had mentioned.

A month went by and I got no call from Gordon Rael. I decided to call the unpleasant guy who had threatened me with a lawsuit if I hadn't complied. He had taken my business cards that were my only proof that I was ever in *Playboy*. He gave me the number of the legal department in Chicago. I left a message and told them I still hadn't received anything from them. This opened a can of worms. They had never heard of my situation and started checking websites to see who might be using my pictures. I tried to explain the entire thing. I hadn't sold any of the pictures. I had just signed them for friends, family, and fans. She was very nice and told me they were quite strict on the use of the logo. Not only could I not use the logo on the picture, I couldn't use the picture either.

Note: I have never heard from her again, which is a good thing. Bruce offered his opinion that if I was sufficiently scared by this latest turn of events the release of my memoir could be worse. Could I handle it? I guess we'll find out. I hired the best entertainment lawyer out of New York to review my book before it was published. I had to leave out a lot of things I wished I could have put in, but he was trying to keep me out of trouble so I guess we'll see!

As for Kim, she decided to call Hef again a few weeks later. After she worked herself up into making the call she thought of reasons to say why she was calling when he got on the line and thought of asking him for a referral for a job interview. Not really needing one, just wanting some reason to call. She called up, and Hef got on the phone and she asked him if she could use him as a referral for a job application. He said *no way*!

She said, "Then is there any way you could give me a job around the mansion?"

He said, "No, I can't help you." He actually laughed at her. She said that she missed him and wanted to see him again, and he was much colder this time. She knew it was over. The conversation was short. A month went by without any word from Hef. She grew more upset and unsettled.

She said, "I was played by an old man."

She began to become angry because she did write him a letter on the first night when she went home with him that she wanted to be a Playmate and that she wanted to be part of *Playboy*. She did not sleep with him till the third date as they say, and he had a chance to know that she wanted him for the reasons of being in the magazine. She did not hide her feelings. She put them down on a piece of paper saying really what she expected. Finally in desperation she decided to write him a letter, and about what it said.

Dear Hef,

After waiting day after day for you to call me, I have had time to check out wireimage.com and look at the Hugh Hefner areas. I realize by looking at the pictures of Sherrie who got to be invited to the Super Bowl XXXVII, the Carmen Electra and Dave Navarro engagement party, The Surreal life viewing party . . . all of these events I was dating and sleeping with you but not invited to these events—only sex nights. I realize you never intended on having me as part of your bunch, but I was good enough to have sex with. My question to you is I had unprotected sex with you on the thought that we had made a connection, but I see know that even though we did, the color of my skin and hair made me not fit into the picture. I understand this perfectly, but Hef, can you at least put me in Special Editions, Cyber Girl, Playmate, something. I feel that I deserve it since my intentions were love, and yours were only sexual.

Love,
Kim

Hef's written response was not the one Kim wanted. He said to her "I didn't initiate our relationship; you did. You are the one who wanted to spend time with me not the other way around. Because I let you come upstairs with us you seem to think I am obligated to you in other ways. I find this very inappropriate, unattractive behavior, and a real turn-off. You seem to see yourself as a victim of some sort. It isn't the color of your skin or hair that is a problem—it is your personality. I'll continue to invite you to parties as long as you behave yourself. But if I get any more communications like this forget it."

Kim did not go to his birthday party because she was so embarrassed by the response she got from Hef. She figured that she would go to the next one.

When the next one came around she called up the mansion and talked to Jenny. She told Jenny her name and asked if she was on the list for the next party. She said no that she was not on the list. Kim asked if she could ask Hef if she could be on the list.

Later that day Jenny called her back and said, "Kim, I just talked to Hef and he said, *no*. So the answer is no. Maybe next time in the future. Okay? Bye-Bye." That was it. She was so upset.

She called me and said, "I'm banned. You might as well have just called me and told me that I was banned. I don't know why they didn't."

She continued, "Yeah, I'm banned. I fucked him for nothing. For nothing—okay? I'm better off fucking some old guy that farts himself that, you know, leaves you $90 million like Anna Nicole Smith. Oh God, what a waste."

Chapter Nine

Okay let's recap. I have just been to the mansion and very plainly been, as they call it, on the "casting couch in LA" "either spread or fled" whatever else slang you want to put on it. But there's more to my parting with *Playboy* than that. The plot thickens.

I was in L.A., and I was at a place where the woman does expert eyebrow tattooing and eyelash dying. I was referred by Tina Jordan and Michelle the gal that I stayed out in the guest house with at the Playboy Mansion. I used her because I admired the work she did for many of the *Playboy* models. The woman working on me told me about her new location opening up and that Tina Jordan and Michelle were showing up that evening at 4:00 for a photo shoot and that she would really appreciate it if I would show up to be one of the models because I had great skin, great figure and that she would trade me out some services for doing it. She knew I was friends with both Tina and Michelle because both of them had referred me to her salon. I was so excited and thrilled and told her that I definitely would.

I headed back home right then because I had no makeup on or anything cute to wear and the salon asked me to wear something sexy. Bruce and I headed back to Malibu, and I spent over 2½ hours getting all dolled up with eyelashes, full hair, etc. and then headed to her new location for the photo shoot. When I walked in I expected to find many models, but I just found Michelle and Tina in the waiting room. They seemed so excited to see me, and I was excited to see them. They called Tina into the other room to start taking photos of her. We all moved over because Bruce had been sitting on the floor because the couch we were all sitting on only held three people, without Tina sitting down he could move up to the couch.

We started chatting as if Bruce was not there, talking about our careers, and she told me about getting new head shots and that she was planning on being on a soap opera and that she was doing many auditions. I showed her my new Zed cards that I had just completed and my 8 x 10 black and white shot. She said she really liked them. I mentioned her hair looked great, she said she removed her extensions and had changed her hair color to more of a brown because to get on soap operas you aren't taken seriously if you are a blonde. She told me about how she had some illness that she ended up in the emergency room during the same day at the Golden Globes.

"Really? I was at the Golden Globes after party at the Beverly Hilton and when I was leaving I saw Hef and all of his girls leaving." This was the truth. The only part that I did not mention was that I could not get in through the guards. I just happened to be hanging out trying to think of another way to try and get in when Hef and his gang was coming out at the same time.

Anyhow, she said that was the day that she was in the emergency room and did not get to go. She said it was the only thing exciting that they got to do and she missed it.

I said "You guys do all kinds of fun things all of the time."

She rolled her eyes and sighed. "Not really."

"You guys are always getting to go places that are really cool."

She said, "Not really."

"The Oscars!"

She said, "We are watching it at the mansion on the big screen."

I said, "All of the parties…all of the famous people at the mansion that come to film and visit!" I mean, if I could have had that life without succumbing to Hef's orgies, I would have. Who wouldn't?

She rolled her eyes again. She then asked me if I was going to the birthday party. I told her no.

She said, "That one is pretty small and boring."

I said that wasn't the reason—I just told Bruce that I was not going to go. I said he has sat at home for the last year as I had explored my dream—and seen the ugly side of "the business."

I added, "I saw Amber in Malibu about a week ago at a bar."

"Oh?"

"What's the real reason that she doesn't live at the mansion anymore. I had heard she was mad because Hef had not made her a playmate and she was sick of him promising so she finally just moved out?"

"I don't know. I think that's probably it."

"I also heard that each of you get to invite four guests to the parties and she was selling them."

"She was. She was actually selling mine, too."

" I wish you had let me know because I would have loved to be able to bring Bruce."

"Amber was selling them for $1500 a piece."

I said, "I would have paid $2000." I told her that it was a $1000 a ticket to just get Bruce into the Playboy Super bowl party in San Diego and it was not even at the Mansion. She did not say anything to my response. She started telling me how broke she was and how everything was costing so much money, head shots, pictures, etc. She then started talking about her daughter needing this and that. She then got called to the back room for shooting. She turned around before leaving the room and said, "Call me, here is my number?"

I smiled. She smiled. I just shook my head in agreement. I was so excited. I was not going to have to miss the birthday party after all. I was going to get to bring Bruce. The look we exchanged was one of understanding. She needed money for her daughter, for her life, and I was willing to pay for the ticket in order to let the love of my life have a glimpse at the strange, glitzy world I had been privy to.

I was the last one for the photo shoot, and when I came back out from the shoot both Michelle and Tina were gone. Michelle had told Vida that she was in a hurry because she had to pick up her daughter. A few days later, Kim and I were already planning on what we were going to wear to the birthday party assuming that I was now going to be at the event with Bruce. Bruce had already picked out what he was going to wear to the mansion based on the conversation with Michelle. He had Playboy bunny boxers and a t-shirt with a picture of Hugh Hefner smoking a cigar.

I said "Hi Michelle. It's Jill Ann. I promise that I will not tell anyone, ever. I'll give you $2,000 to let Bruce get into the mansion for the birthday party. I know you need the money and it would mean a great deal to Bruce to get to go. Please call me ####."

I crossed my heart, and I figured it was a done deal. I figured that I would get a call back from her to exchange the money and if she had chickened out or changed her mind she would call and say no. I didn't hear from her. I called Kim telling her that Michelle had not called back. She said not to worry that often she did not answer her phone when she was at the mansion. A few days went by, and I was thinking about calling Michelle again.

The phone rang early one morning. An unfamiliar voice said, "Hello. I need to speak to Jill Ann Spaulding."

I said, "Speaking."

She said, "This is Marilyn Grabowski, Hef's personal secretary, and I am calling to uninvite you to Hef's birthday party and any other party that Jenny might call you to tell you about."

I said, "Okay. Why?"

She said that it was because of my recent message left with Michelle. It turned out that Michelle had "brought it to Hef's attention and he is appalled that you would do something so underhanded as to get someone into his party."

I said "Okay. Well, I guess it was a misunderstanding because I felt that Michelle brought up the whole situation. May I at least explain to you what exactly happened?"

She said, "Go ahead."

I explained the whole thing—about me, Michelle, and Tina Jordan and the photo shoot. Marilyn then suddenly asked if Tina Jordan was involved in the whole situation. I said no she had nothing to do with it. I then explained the entire conversation that I had with Michelle just as I've outlined here. I said that I must have misunderstood, and I said that the punishment of never being invited again seemed pretty harsh. A simple "We don't appreciate this— Don't do it again—We don't allow this—Hef is disappointed" would have been appropriate. I asked her to please tell Hef my side of the story and to reconsider that it was not premeditated.

She said, "This is Hef's confirmed decision." I felt backed into a corner. I was stunned. I was also shocked that Michelle would do such a thing. I knew treachery at the mansion existed, but this was unbelievable.

I lashed out. I guess the hypocrisy of it all was finally getting to me. I was hoping that maybe it would make Hef reconsider or something. I don't know. I just knew I had done wrong by telling her how I really felt.

A few hours went by, and I had already called my entire family, as well as Kim, and I was so upset. Bruce felt awful because he felt it was his fault. It wasn't, of course. I just got so upset I decided to call back the mansion and discuss it with them again. I asked for Marilyn Grabowski.

The woman who answered said that Marilyn Grabowski was in a meeting with Hef. I asked if she could leave a message for her.

"It is really important," I said.

"What is it in reference to?"

I said, "It is concerning me never being allowed to go to another party at the Mansion again."

She said, "Okay" and I started explaining that I had no intentions on doing anything that would upset Hef, and that I did not think offering money to get Bruce into a party was this terrible. I started explaining that I had paid $1005 to go to the New Orleans Party for *Playboy* and that I paid $1000 just to get Bruce in to the *Playboy* party for the Super Bowl, that I paid $1000 a day to get Bruce into the *Playboy* Golf Scramble at the Playboy Mansion. I did not realize that it was going to upset him this much and that I did not mean anything by it.

She was very nice and sided with me, she said she understood how much pressure that girls got to bring their boyfriends to the parties and that it was understandable and many people had offered money to get their friends and boyfriends in. I thanked her for her time and said that I felt the punishment was extreme. She agreed and said she would relay the message to Marilyn. No one ever called back. It was this very week that I started to write my book.

Why? I finally realized that all of my ties with *Playboy* were no longer, that there was no more hope, no more second chance. That this was it. I had nothing to lose. I suddenly was able to take a step back, as well, and look at what was going on in the bright light of what it is. I found an editor who was interested in my book. I had scheduled an appointment to meet with the editor in person. That week prior to meeting with her, I thought of sending a copy of the book to Hef. Why? was it blackmail on my part? No. I thought of many different reactions, and dreams crossed my mind; he would either have one of his goons kill me, silence me, or pay me off. Maybe he would want the book written to boost his ego. He probably wouldn't care, or maybe he would put me in his magazine in exchange for me not writing the book. God, would he have me destroyed? Or do the opposite, maybe even make me a Playmate. Don't think that all the various results of my determination to tell my story did not cross my mind many times.

I feel the fear of the other consequences or him letting one of his regular girls beat me to writing the book because he might as well have someone that slept with him write it instead of it coming out through me. But I didn't send him the book ahead of time.

Bruce pressed to the editor why it needed to be written—and quickly before the word got out. *Playboy* has such a power over these girls that they need to know what they are getting into and the soul they will have to sell. He said he had no concept of why I would still want to be in this man's magazine after all that I had gone through but that there was that driving force. It's confronting an icon of sexuality.

Epilogue

This whole experience was devastating and disillusioning. The journey that had been my dream since I was very young was over. My family, friends, and companion had all encouraged and supported me. I had worked hard, suffered the pain of surgeries, paid hundreds of dollars on promotion, and I wonder with what I am left.

I am still the little girl who dreams of being well known and well loved—of filling that void to prove to myself that I am worthy of love. For all the girls that dream of being a *Playboy* model or anything like it I would caution them to approach it from a business standpoint. The "casting couch" is too expensive. I will say that all the young girls giving "it" up to achieve the goal have ruined it for those of us wanting to retain our integrity, morals, and ethics. My path would have been completely different if I had been willing to give up my values on life and love. This doesn't mean to say that those unfortunates forced into a temporary lifestyle to stay alive are worthy of disdain. Survival is paramount, and hope is the one thing that keeps the heart alive.

I realized that my age was not the problem because one of the girls who was in bed with Hugh Hefner the two nights I was upstairs was 36-years old. I watched her have sex with Hef both nights. At 36-years old she made Playmate of the month®. I said no to sex with him and I feel this is why I didn't make Playmate of the month® or anything in the *Playboy* Magazine. So ladies, itwasn't my age, it was my lack of the sexual participation. My opinion is I would have had to become a hired sex slave for twice a week participation for as long as he saw fit or wanted me; waiting day upon day trying to please his every wish in hopes that I would not be cut and ultimately make Playmate like most of the girlfriends that had come before me. As for the beautiful Platinum Diamond *Playboy* Necklace. I got mine. How? I found out the manufacturer of the exact same ones that Hef gives his girlfriends and playmates, and I drove to the office myself. I purchased the Official Diamond Platinum Playboy necklace for $750. It was the same amount I got paid for my *Playboy* Shoot so in some ways *Playboy* paid for it except I had Bruce put it around my neck instead of Hef.

When I look back, I think of the money I spent on the "casting couch." Gordon Rael? He never sent me on a single other shoot or any other work after I spent all that money on photos that supposedly had to be "just right." There are men out there waiting to hook innocent young girls, girls with stars in their eyes.

Ultimately, when you look in the mirror, and I mean really look—wherever you are in life—were the sacrifices you made for the furs, expensive cars, jewelry and glamour, and attention worth the price? When your beauty fades, and it will despite your unwillingness to accept it, will you be able to look back on your decisions and be comfortable in your skin? Will the price tag I have tried to show you that was presented to me be worth it?

You decide girls, gals, women and ladies and even guys. Which path will you choose? I made it up the stairs and had the courage to walk down, out the gate and home to those who love me and will be with me always.

A few interesting things that I read that I wanted to share;

Quoted from *Inside the Playboy Mansion the video* "There are no skeletons in my life. My life's an open book."

Quoted from *USA Today*, Hef says "They're girlfriends," he says. "It's a typical relationship, times seven." He then later in the interview goes on to say, "It's very reciprocal. I don't think there's any exploitation going on. It obviously benefits all concerned, or everybody wouldn't be here and so happy."

Quoted from *The Washington Post* by Peter Carlson, Hef said the following; "Chronologically, I'm seventy-seven, but in reality I'm a very young man. I may be wearing this old face and body but I'm still the same guy. Well, I am still the same guy. ...Power has not corrupted me. I have not been jaded."

Vanity Fair March 2001, Hef refers to his girlfriends to the reporter "Meet Girl Scout Troop 36." In the same article, one of the girls, Cathi O'Malley says that, "Mostly it's like being at your grandma's house... Except for the zoo." During the interview one of the butlers comes in, and she asks "Did a doctor call for me today? I went to the gynecologist for the first time. And he said he would call if there was anything wrong—so no news is good news."

Cathi announces brightly "Hey, guys, I can drink tonight!"

Katie Lohmann rolls her eyes. "Oh, great."

"I had to take antibiotics," says Cathi, "and I was sick for a while, and I couldn't drink."

"And wasn't able to participate in extracurricular activities!" Regina says. "Clap on, clap off, the clapper!" Katie snorts. "Hello? Chlamydia?"

Vanity Fair, March 2001, Hef is quoted as saying, "I've created this incredible machine that brings to me the most beautiful young women in the world, and they come already wanting to be in the magazine or somehow a part of my life. . . . There can be some territorial things between them—we're sorting through some of that right now—but mostly it's working out very well."

In that same article, Buffy Tyler is quoted, "It's hard when you come from a small town and you don't know what to do and how to meet people, and you don't know where to go or what to do and then, sure enough, hey, what do you know. I'm here," Buffy says. "Pretty cool. You know, all my friends used to be, like, O.K., Buffy, whatever – and I'm like, you watch, I'll get there—."

Marksfriggin.com reports, Hef was interviewed by Howard Stern on February 2, 2001, and he says he hardly ever uses a condom though. He says he always has a close-knit relationship with one or more people and he doesn't feel he needs a condom.

Marksfriggin.com reports Tina Jordan was interviewed by Howard Stern on 4/1/03 and she said she doesn't know why Hef's girlfriends lie about not sleeping with Hef. She said they all do and doesn't understand why they'd lie about that. She said she made close to $100,000 a year during her stay.

Globe, December 30, 2003, "Hef has five other regular gal-pals, Girls literally throw themselves at him every time we go out," she says. "He often invited one to come back home to bed with us."

Hefner is quoted in *Hot Stuff* as saying, "Britney would make a great girlfriend." (Referring to Britney Spears).

"When you have sex with someone, you are having sex with everyone they have had sex with for the last ten years, and everyone they and their partners have had sex with for the last ten years." C. Everett Koop, M.D., former U.S. Surgeon General.

These facts and Common Sexually Transmitted Disease table were provided by The Women's Center of Northwest Indiana

Fact: **Oral sex, anal sex, vaginal sex, mutual** masturbation . . . It's all sex. STD's are often passed by skin to skin contact.

Fact: **About 85% of women and 40% of men infected with Chlamydia don't know it . . . yet!**

Fact: **The CDC estimates that 900,000 living Americans are infected**

with HIV, and the majority doesn't know it.
   Fact: **About one third of infertility in women is caused by STD's.**
   Fact: **One in every five Americans over the age of eleven has geni-
tal herpes.**

COMMON SEXUALLY TRANSMITTED DISEASES

DISEASE	EFFECTS	COMMENTS
Chlamydia	Causes PID, chronic pain, infertility, problems during pregnancy.	Over 4 million new cases each year.
Gonorrhea	Causes PID, chronic pain, infertility, ectopic pregnancy, arthritis.	1.3 million New cases per year. Some strains are resistant to treatment.
Genital Human Papillomavirus (HPV)	Causes genital warts, cervical neoplasia; linked to cancer of the cervix.	Over 1 million reported causes per year.
Herpes (HSV-2)	Painful blisters around sex organs; produces fever, enlarged lymph glands, flu-like symptoms.	Almost 500,000 new cases reported each year. INCURABLE
Hepatitis B	Causes cirrhosis and cancer.	300,000 new cases reported each year.
AIDS	FATAL; INCURABLE	Estimated 40 million worldwide by the year 2000.
Syphilis	Leads to blindness, heart disease, nervous disorders, insanity, tumors and death.	Over 100,000 reported cases per year.

Information below provided by "The American Health Association"
American Social Health Association

Sexually Transmitted Diseases

STDs are infections that can be spread by having sex with another person who is infected. If you have sex with someone who has an STD, you can get it too. Many people who have an STD don't know it. They may look healthy, but they still could have a STD. Some people won't tell you, even if they know. Look through the list below to find more information about a particular STD.

AIDS and HIV -Human immunodeficiency virus or HIV is a virus that attacks the immune system resulting in Acquired Immunodeficiency Syndrome, or AIDS.

Chancroid - A treatable bacterial infection that causes painful sores.

Chlamydia - A treatable bacterial infection that can scar the fallopian tubes affecting a woman's ability to have children.

Crabs - Also known as pediculosis pubis, crabs are parasites or bugs that live on the pubic hair in the genital area.

Gonorrhea - A treatable bacterial infection of the penis, vagina or anus that causes pain, or burning feeling as well as a pus-like discharge. Also known as "the clap".

Hepatitis - A disease that affects the liver. There are more than four types. A and B are the most common.

Herpes - Genital herpes is a recurrent skin condition that can cause skin irritations in the genital region (anus, vagina, penis).

Human Papillomavirus / Genital Warts - Human papillomavirus (HPV) is a virus that affects the skin in the genital area, as well as a female's cervix. Depending on the type of HPV involved, symptoms can be in the form of wart-like growths, or abnormal cell changes.

Nongonococcal Urethritis (NGU) Nongonococcal urethritis (or NGU) is a treatable bacterial infection of the urethra (the tube within the penis) often times associated with chlamydia.

Pelvic Inflammatory Disease - An infection of the female reproductive organs by chlamydia, gonorrhea or other bacteria. Also known as PID.

Scabies - Scabies is a treatable skin disease that is caused by a parasite.

Syphilis - A treatable bacterial infection that can spread throughout the body and affect the heart, brain, nerves. Also known as "syph".

When coming to L.A., when trying to make it as a star, all I can say is consider this book. Consider the facts listed. Think beyond the next party, the next night out. Think of your life. Sometimes dreams can be illusions. The mansion . . . upstairs . . . is nothing more than that.

Related information can be found at:
www.playboy.com/help/email.html

This is where I got my pictures accepted for Playboy.com. This is the place you should send your photos for submission.

Chicago Office
680 North Lake Shore Drive
Chicago, Illinois 60611
Attention: Picture Submission/Playmate Candidate
Phone: 312.751.8000
Fax: 312.751.2818

This is where I called to set up a Playmate Test Shoot and where I suggest you send your photos also:

Playboy Studio West
2112 Broadway
Santa Monica, California 90404
Attention: Picture Submission/Playmate Candidate
Phone: 310.264.6600
Fax: 310.264.1944

Letters that were sent to Hef and from Hugh Hefner:

Playboy Mansion West
10236 Charing Cross Road
Los Angeles, California 90024

I would love to hear what you thought about my book. Please send any reviews or letters to:

Jill Ann Spaulding
3454 E. Southern Avenue #104
Mesa, Arizona 85204
(this is not my living address so please give me
a few weeks to respond to your letter)

or email me at
Jillann@Jillann.com

My Friend Jill

I have a beautiful friend her name is Jill,
You will find her to be a great thrill.

Her last name is Spaulding,
I guarantee she is not balding.
And her heart is as golden as her long beautiful hair.
If you dare she loves to share,
Her sweet personality and warm smile.

As she passes,
Don't be mistaken she will leave you thinking for awhile.
Her body voluptuous as well as stunning,
Some when seeing her comes running.....

I find she is misunderstood by many,
What she has to offer is definitely plenty.....
I'm not talking about what is most vivid,
Because for some they are livid.

The inner part of her makes her shine,
Don't be blind,
So make sure you take the time.

Then,
You too can say you have a beautiful friend name Jill.
Who will be a wonderful thrill.....
To know and say you know,
Such as I.

Betty Kennedy
6-7-04

Printed in the United States
20750LVS00006B/302